Blossom Culp and the Sleep of Death

RICHARD PECK

BLOSSOM CULP
AND THE
SLEEP OF DEATH

DELACORTE PRESS/NEW YORK

Published by
Delacorte Press
1 Dag Hammarskjold Plaza
New York, N.Y. 10017

Library of Congress Cataloging-in-Publication Data
Peck, Richard
Blossom Culp and the sleep of death.
Summary: Blossom, high-school freshman and possessor
of "second sight," helps an Egyptian princess, dead for
3500 years, to regain her tomb, and in addition saves a
suffragette schoolteacher from losing her job in 1914.
[1. Space and time—Fiction. 2. Schools—Fiction.
3. Extrasensory perception—Fiction. 4. Egypt—Civilization—To 332 B.C.—Fiction] I. Title.
PZ7.P338B   1986   [Fic]
ISBN 0-385-29433-6
Library of Congress Catalog Card Number: 85-16188

To Carolyn and Bob Kimbell, in long friendship

Prologue

OUT AT THE EDGE OF BLUFF CITY WHERE I reside there's an open pasture screened from the road by a stand of trees. This is a hidden place, so don't expect to run across it by chance. But if you concentrate, you can see it in your mind's eye. There, whipped by November's chill winds, are the wretched remains of a traveling tent show. It was a two-bit sort of circus—bankrupt, abandoned, and left over from last summer.

As times are always hard for the traveling-tent-show business, its unknown proprietors dumped everything along about Labor Day and fled just ahead of their creditors and other public-spirited citizens. Now in November nature's reclaiming the sad leavings. A slanting tentpole stands against the weather, and a tent flap flaps. A string of bobbing lights have long since flickered out, and if there was a lion at all with this particular outfit, his roar has long since echoed away to silence.

The circus had side shows, of course: one trained-dog act, one freak, one girly, and one of ancient mysteries. Their posters are down now, with all the colors run together. A passing cow has made a mess of one.

Little is left as winter draws in, for remote as this location is, a vandal has discovered it. Under cover of night a vandal's grabby hands have sorted through this desolation and carried away an assortment of valuables.

But listen to me. Left there forlorn beneath the rotting canvas lies a secret old as time, half buried in the dismal debris. Dry and leathery, it lies in wait, bearing an old grudge. A secret lies alone and lonely out on that littered prairie, and secrets will out or my name isn't Blossom Culp. Remember this eerie scene, for it bears on my story.

1

IT'S A WELL-KNOWN FACT THAT EVERYBODY has their talents. Some people have a natural ability to play the banjo or do needlepoint or call hogs.

Some are endowed with beauty or wealth. And sometimes, unfairly, with both.

Some people are popular, though you pay for that gift with your privacy.

My name is Blossom Culp, and none of the above applies to me.

But I have a talent or two, though certain people would deny it. I come from a long line of fortune-tellers, wart-healers, and finders of lost articles. There's gypsy blood flowing in my family, and that has kept us on our toes and moving. And so my supernatural talents are natural to me.

It's been given to me by Forces Unknown to unlock the heavy doors of Time and enter history past and future. Life is short, but I've roamed far from mine.

While interesting and educational, my talent only works part time. Something will set me off, and there I go wandering into other times entirely, like a lost sheep. I'm always on a mission, of course, serving the needs of a soul somewhere in torment.

This Gift has its drawbacks, but then I've always had a full share of drawbacks myself. Though the past and future are often open books to me, I have more trouble than most getting through the present. It was this difficult present that was much on my mind here a while back.

If you're stuck in school like the rest of us, you'll notice how things always seem to go downhill every year after Halloween. All the pranks and costumes of that ghastly season were behind us. There seemed nothing to look forward to but Thanksgiving, which is far from a feast around my house. And Christmas vacation was too distant to count.

We of the freshman class here at Bluff City High School had made our mark on Halloween of the year 1914 by running a haunted house as a charity event. While the entire class likes to keep me in my place, I came in quite handy at our haunted house as an expert fortune-teller and general witch-of-all-work.

But as quick as people have no more use for you, they'll drop you like a hot potato. And Halloween was over. The construction-paper punkins were curling on the bulletin boards, and the twists of orange and black crêpe paper festooning the halls hung in tatters. As far as I could see, there was no

cure for this tiresome season. As November deep-
ened, I began to feel like a leftover bird who's
forgotten to migrate.

Being freshmen just naturally magnifies every
problem. The boys were all growing taller but no
wiser. The girls were growing restless. All in all, it
was like being locked up with a bunch of jittery
jailbirds.

As it happened, a few of the freshmen were
turning to new activities to put some life into this
dreary month. But since I was the class outcast,
nobody told me a thing. I can often get a clearer
view of other worlds than of this one.

I found time hanging so heavy on my hands that
I about decided to apply myself to my schoolwork.
I'm a quick study and strictly on my own most of
the time, which helps you to concentrate. While
the boys squirmed like spotted pups and the girls
passed notes to everybody but me, I kept myself
alert.

In biology class we were still cutting up worms.
In English Miss Blankenship had just given up trying to cram the play *Hamlet* down our throats.
Now she was about to try a book on us called *A Tale
of Two Cities*, which as I understand it deals with
the French Revolution of 1789. Considering her
age, Miss Blankenship could no doubt give us an
eyewitness account of that particular event herself.

Her years of servitude as a teacher have thinned
out her hair considerably. When she cast *Hamlet*

aside and took up the new book, the rays of the overhead light gleamed on the stretched skin of her half-bald head.

" '*It was the best of times,*' " Miss Blankenship blared, rattling the window glass, " '*it was the worst of times.*' "

Several students looked up in alarm. They'd been expecting her to start raving out of her head, and this seemed to be the day. Up the aisle from me Ione Williams looked across at Nola Nirider and tapped a finger on her temple.

" '. . . *It was the season of Light, it was the season of Darkness, it was the spring of hope, it was the winter of despair.*' "

When it dawned on the class that Miss Blankenship was only quoting from literature, they went back to their own activities.

"And so," she intoned, "did Mr. Charles Dickens begin his epic story of one of the most horrible moments in the tide of human events!"

Determined to win us over to Charles Dickens's way of thinking, Miss Blankenship held up a withered finger. "*Hark,* children, at the ominous sound of the tumbrils rattling over the cobblestones of Paris, and *woe* to their human cargo!"

As I understand it a tumbril is a two-wheeled cart used to transport high-class society people to the guillotine to have their heads chopped off.

"And *hark* at the fatal sound of the razor-sharp blade whistling down upon the fair necks of the French aristocracy!"

"Ouch!" cried Alexander Armsworth aloud. He's a kid of my close acquaintance, and I generally sit in the desk behind him. Me and him have more in common than he cares to admit, and I'm often nearer him than he knows.

Peering over his shoulder I saw that Alexander had been passing the time by sharpening a pencil point with his pocket knife. A small pyramid of wood shavings on his desk was turning blood-red before our very eyes because his knife had slipped and sliced a thin patch of skin and cuticle off his thumb.

Miss Blankenship shot him a glance, but she seemed to be carried away by tumbrils. "And *hark* at the sickening sound of wellborn heads dropping into the *blood-soaked* basket!"

Letty Shambaugh's head drooped suddenly. She was sitting across the aisle from me also monitoring Alexander. Now she was looking down at her own bosom, wondering where it was.

From the front of the room I daresay it looked like Letty was taking careful notes on the flyleaf of *A Tale of Two Cities.* Even while her eyes searched the ruffles of her blouse for something more substantial, she held a little gold inkpen poised in her hand.

I let one of my eyes drift over to read these so-called notes she was making. As near as I could figure they read as follows:

S.T. & B.F.S. Monthly Meeting
Agenda
  I. Grooming Tips and Beauty Secrets
     A. Our figures—what to do?
     B. Complexion Hints (if time)
 II. Entertainment
     A. Refreshments (tell Mother)
     B. Ouija board
III. Old Business
     A. Boys
     B. Boys
 IV. New Business
     A. Annual Homecoming Parade Float
     B. ?

This was as far as she'd gotten, but it was a long way from the French Revolution.

I'll say one thing and one thing only for Letty Shambaugh. Small though her mind is, she keeps it busy. Letty finds it hard to work education into her full schedule, as she's president of both the freshman class and a private club of girls called the Sunny Thoughts and Busy Fingers Sisterhood. This particular gang wastes no time in holding elections, because Letty is president for life. Besides, Letty doesn't approve of members of the female sex voting in elections of any sort, as I was soon to learn.

The Sunny Thoughts and Busy Fingers Sisterhood girls have been looking down on me ever since fourth grade, when I hit town, and I'll have to live longer than Miss Blankenship even to darken their door. Or so it seemed on that dull November day.

It did not faze me. A club is what you belong to when you can't make your own plans. I'll have to admit, though, that one thing about Letty stuck in my craw. She's sweet on Alexander Armsworth.

Whenever she looks his way, Letty's little liquid eyes turn to large limpid pools. Being a boy, Alexander is fool enough to fall for her if I don't keep my wits about him.

I suppose that some would say these two are well suited. Alexander is one of the handsomest boys in our class, and Letty's considered pretty if you like the type. I can tell you this much: she is sure stuck on herself. In a special pocket on the inside of her notebook cover she carried a small hand mirror and jerked it out during every class to admire herself. When she thought nobody was looking, one of her little hands stole up and pinched both her cheeks to give them rosebuds. It was a sickening display.

Another thing that Alexander and Letty have in common is that they're both from well-to-do families socially prominent in this city. Letty's paw is the sole owner of the Select Dry Goods Company, and Alexander's is a big-time house builder at present excavating several entire streets of new houses. This makes both the Shambaughs and the Armsworths aristocratic families in these parts.

If this was the Paris of 1789 instead of the Bluff City of 1914 I expect both Alexander and Letty would be tied in a tumbril and fated to lose their heads, though not over each other.

Letty noticed how one of my eyes was drinking in the agenda she'd been drawing up. I couldn't make head or tail of it myself, but she banged down the cover on *A Tale of Two Cities* with a report like gunfire.

At the same moment Alexander's hand shot up to interrupt Miss Blankenship.

"Yes, Alexander." She sighed. "What now?"

"I have had a serious accident and better report to the nurse before lockjaw sets in!" He put up the hand with the sliced thumb on it. He'd trained a thin line of blood to trickle down his wrist, where it made a small blob on his cuff.

"Very well, Alexander." Miss Blankenship rubbed her forehead. "You will not be missed."

He was already up in a crouch and aiming himself at the door like every minute could be his last.

"*Hark,* children," Miss Blankenship continued, "at the footsteps of the ragtag mob ringing over the cobblestones of Paris half-starved and hungry now for *blood,* not bread!"

The bell rang, drowning her words, and the entire class swarmed toward the door like a determined bunch of hungry French peasants. Personally, I can't see why everybody's in such an almighty rush to get out of one class when five minutes later we'll be in another one. We're cooped up here all day anyhow, and we might as well be in one cell as another.

Letty can't be hurried either. She's not fond of rules she hasn't made herself, and so she was organizing her books and patting the large taffeta bow that holds up her back hair. Then when she swept up her books and swung her little knees into the aisle, one of those things happened that can brighten your whole day.

Her hand mirror slipped free of the notebook and fell to the floor, shattering. I grinned widely.

Letty clutched her throat and very nearly noticed me. Responsible rumor has reached her that I'm gifted with a Power or two beyond the everyday mortal. While Alexander Armsworth works hard to stifle his own Powers and keeps quiet about them, I don't believe in hiding my light under a bushel.

Letty never has been entirely sure about the extent of my Powers. For all she knows, I may have the Evil Eye and can put a hex on her. She has good reason to believe I can tell a true fortune if I'm in the mood. She even suspects I'm saving back a talent or two for a special occasion, and maybe I am.

But accidents will happen, and Letty's mirror was one of them. On the other hand it would certainly do her no harm to think I'd been working a little light witchcraft on her to keep in practice. When I was sure she'd notice, I let my eyeballs roll back in my head and showed her my whites. Though this is one of my smaller skills, it never fails to leave a deep impression. Letty gasped.

Even when I'm looking square at you, I'm no oil painting. I let my eyeballs roll forward again and blinked them back into place. "I make that seven years bad luck," I remarked, "even with time off for good behavior."

Then I loped off up the aisle, leaving her to draw her own conclusions. Behind me came the sound of grinding glass as Letty stamped her sharp little heel into the remains of her mirror.

This welcome little diversion made a nice change in the schoolday. But when we all got to history class in the next period, us freshmen were in for a change that would shake us to our foundations.

2

EVEN IN AN UP-TO-DATE INSTITUTION LIKE Bluff City High School, problems will arise. We had one here a while back with a history teacher, name of Mr. Ambrose Lacy. Though he was a fine figure of a man, his character was bad. Come to find out he'd trifled with the affections of one or two of the lady teachers. Once in a while a teacher has to be run out of town. We run him out.

There was now a hole in the history department, plugged on a temporary basis by a string of substitute teachers. We freshmen made none of them welcome, and so they came and went.

On the day in question we entered history to find the classroom without a grown-up in sight. Finding ourselves in possession of the place, us freshmen ran riot.

The girls contented themselves with milling around and conversing at the top of their lungs. The boys went into action. A few of them upended their desks and formed what looked like an Indian wigwam at the rear of the room, where they seemed to take up residence.

A brawnier bunch run by a big bruiser named Belcher Cunningham began chasing Collis Ledbetter around the room and cutting him off in corners. Collis Ledbetter's crime is that he's the smallest kid in the class of either sex. Quick though he was, his tormentors soon fell on him. Four of them had him by the shirt collar and the heels and were lugging him across the room like a bundle.

When Collis saw he was being carried in the direction of the window, he commenced shrieking in a high, hopeless voice. One of his captors whipped out a pocket handkerchief, none too clean, and stuffed it into Collis's mouth.

Being strictly modern the high school has a complicated set of blinds rigged up at every window. Lucky for Collis these window blinds are of high-quality canvas, for the gang intended to roll him up into the blind on the upper window and leave him there.

Working together Belcher and his boys soon drew down the blind to its full length and laid the wiggling Collis into it like it was a hammock. He made a fairly tidy package as they rolled him over in three layers of canvas. By pulling in unison on the cords they began to wind the blind up and Collis in it. Though it was hard work, boys will go to any length on a job like this.

Wringing wet, Collis wouldn't weigh sixty

pounds. Even so, the blind sagged and threatened to split. And though he is a small kid, he made quite a bulge in it. Still, the other boys pulled together, and Collis rolled revolving upward.

When he sensed he was a good ten feet off the floor with no hope of rescue, Collis ceased squirming and ascended to the ceiling in something like dignity. Belcher's boys gave the cords a final jerk and tied them firmly to the hooks provided for that purpose.

They were just turning around in search of a new project when we were all frozen in our tracks. A teacher entered our madhouse, and it was no substitute. You can spot a substitute a mile away. It's written all over their faces, but this was the real thing.

Why she turned us all into pillars of salt I cannot say. As teachers go, she was on the young side and quite a handsome woman in a plain way. She raised neither her hand nor her voice against us. It must have been her eyes that struck us dumb. They were a pair of pale-blue flints striking cold sparks.

You could see she was all business. Her hair was gathered into a no-nonsense knot on the top of her head. The shirtwaist on her fine chest was laid in neat pleats, and her tweedy skirts were of a practical length, clearing her ankles. A sensible band of leather was sewn around the bottom of her skirts to spare her hem, and she wore paper cuffs to save her sleeves. She stood surveying the room until we began to subside. People drifted to their seats. The Indian wigwam at the rear uprighted itself.

Then the new teacher astounded us by reaching into a pocket of her skirt and drawing out a small disc of clear glass. Many of the other teachers favor spectacles of the pince-nez variety. These are two rimmed lenses that clamp over the bridge of the nose and attach to a button on the bosom by a length of black ribbon.

This teacher was altogether different. She raised the single lens to one of her eyes and lodged it there atop her cheekbone. It was a monocle, the first one we'd seen.

The monocle magnified one of her eyes terribly. The flinty blue of her pupil examined her pupils without pity. Evidently she didn't care for what she saw.

"My name is Augusta Fairweather," she said in a cultivated voice of doom.

We shrank.

"You may address me as Miss Fairweather if you are called upon to speak at all."

Never was a woman more poorly named. A storm cloud seemed to form over Miss Fairweather's head, threatening to shed cold sleet all over the room. We sat stunned in meek rows. Hands clasped obediently together on desk tops up and down the aisles.

"I am not accustomed to serving as a teacher in a town this small," she remarked in the same colorless voice.

We were speechless. Bluff City is the biggest burg several of us have ever experienced. I personally have been around, but as I say, I'm different.

"I am not used to country children or country manners," she announced.

Across from me Letty Shambaugh made a strangled sound. The idea that anybody thought she was a country child nearly robbed her of her reason. And I have to admit I couldn't picture Letty wearing a poke bonnet or coming to school by mule or eating her lunch out of a bucket, though I smiled at the thought.

"This is outrageous," Letty hissed to nobody in particular.

"I have come to this out-of-the-way village," Miss Fairweather went on, "to replace your former history teacher. You are lucky to get me on short notice. You will find I am a very different proposition from Mr. Lacy. After all, he was a man." Her nose wrinkled.

But hearing Mr. Lacy's name stirred us. After all, we'd successfully run him out of town.

"History is largely written by men," Miss Fairweather remarked. "This is why it is regularly wrong."

I found that an interesting viewpoint, but Letty murmured, "Unwomanly!" well under her breath. She'd been studying Miss Fairweather from the first moment with blanket disapproval. "Paper cuffs," she muttered. "Whatever next?"

Letty's taste runs to multiple ruffles, wide sashes,

and plenty of lace around the petticoat. She goes around much of the time trussed up like a Valentine card.

Still, Miss Fairweather held us in a grip of steel.

"There are only two rules in this classroom. You will obey them both. The first is that I am the teacher and you are not.

"The second is—"

The door banged back, and Alexander Armsworth came breezing in from the nurse. On his injured thumb was a brown spot of iodine the size of a wart. He was holding this hand aloft and shaking it briskly to take the sting out of it.

The classroom was so silent that Alexander evidently thought he'd lost his hearing. All he wanted to do was show off his wounded thumb, and here we all sat like the living dead in neat rows like a cemetery. As usual he was slow to recover.

Miss Fairweather turned and examined him from the knobs of his boots up his knickered legs and belted jacket to the unformed features of his face. When it dimly dawned on him that we had a new teacher, he found her studying him with two eyes of different sizes, both piercing. He jumped.

"A diller, a dollar, a ten o'clock scholar," Miss Fairweather quoted ruthlessly.

"Who, me?" Alexander said, badly stumped.

"I am Miss Fairweather," she remarked. "You are late."

"Who, me?" Alexander repeated. "I've just come from the—"

"I don't care if you have just come from President Wilson in the White House. Find a seat and take it."

Alexander blundered down a row, looking abused.

"And the second rule of this class," Miss Fairweather flowed on, "is to forget what little history you have learned so far. In this room we will study history as it was lived, not as it has been written about by men."

This was too much for Letty. She skidded out of her seat. "Miss Fairweather, as president of the entire freshman class, I must protest," she said in her businesslike tone. "We have learned plenty of sound history over many long years, and I, for one, want credit for it. Besides, why shouldn't history be written by men? Writing history is hard work, and that is what men are for."

Miss Fairweather's monocle struck a spark of white fire. "Who might you be?"

Letty twitched. She isn't used to being unknown. "Letty Shambaugh, of course," she replied with some spirit. "My mother is the president of the Daughters of the American Revolution, and my papa is—"

"Your parents are not in this class," Miss Fairweather interrupted, "if they ever went to high school at all. Resume your seat."

Letty crumpled.

"Steps must be taken," she hissed loud enough to be heard by the nearest of the S.T. & B.F.S. girls.

But Miss Fairweather only seemed to scan the distant past, saying, "It has taken nearly five thousand years of recorded history to produce you freshmen. And so history has a lot to answer for. I suggest we begin at the beginning. And since you have already studied so much history, let us find out precisely what you know."

Across from me Letty's mind was whirling as she ripped a small lacy handkerchief to shreds in her nervousness.

" 'Four score and seven years ago,' " she muttered, racking her brain, " 'our forefathers brought forth—' "

"Can anyone in this group of scholars tell me which people invented the first calendar?" Miss Fairweather sent the searchlight of her monocle sweeping over us.

Letty leaned forward and poked Harriet Hochhuth sitting ahead of her. "The ancient Romans," Letty hissed into Harriet's ear.

Suddenly inspired, Harriet raised her hand and gave that answer.

"The Romans?" said Miss Fairweather. "Certainly not. How ridiculous."

Harriet wilted, and Letty fell back. If she'd been sure of the answer, she'd have given it herself. "Try the Israelites," Letty hissed, but Harriet wouldn't chance it.

"It was the Egyptians," Miss Fairweather said triumphantly, "on or about the year 4241 B.C." She let that sink in while she continued to scan us.

"Consider the Egyptians. Were these people mere savages who strolled out of their cave dwellings one bright morning and devised a workable calendar? Certainly not. They were already a people of cities and science and much learning."

Miss Fairweather gazed away from us, seeming to see a vision of these proud ancients when our ancestors were still swinging from one tree to the other. I don't mean she had an actual vision. I can always spot such people, as I'm one of them myself. It was only that Miss Fairweather was a real scholarly woman, as well as somewhat sarcastic. These two traits often go hand in hand.

"Oh, well, Egypt," Alexander remarked, just now catching the drift. "We did Egypt back in fourth grade." Unfortunately, his voice carries.

"Did you indeed?" Miss Fairweather said dangerously.

Much encouraged, Alexander nodded. "We had a sand table and made a relief map of the entire Egypt area out of flour and water. I myself colored in the River Nile with green poster paint."

"Ah," said Miss Fairweather, training her monocle on him. "Did you include both the Upper and Lower Kingdoms?"

"We may have," Alexander replied. "We made pyramids out of modeling clay and put them in."

"Modeling clay," Miss Fairweather mused. "What is your name?"

"Alexander Armsworth," he said, ". . . ma'am."

"And how many little clay pyramids did you in-

clude on this accurate map, Alexander Armsworth?"

"We put in three."

"There are eighty pyramids still in existence,"
she said witheringly. "The Egyptians were among
the earliest of the stone-builders. The Great Pyramid of Cheops at Giza three miles southwest of
Cairo covers thirteen acres. A hundred thousand
laborers slaved for twenty years in its construction.
Did you do justice to this significant achievement
in fourth grade, young Armsworth?"

Alexander began to sink.

But an odd thing was happening to me. I could
have sworn we were in for a change of weather.
Somewhere way off I seemed to hear a roll of thunder. The schoolroom lights blinked and went dim,
though nobody noticed. If it hadn't been for torch-
light suddenly flaming, we'd have been cast into
utter darkness. At least I would.

The walls and blackboards seemed to crumble,
and I felt the hot wind of the desert on my face. I
looked back better than four thousand years into
an ancient evening and saw in the dark purple sky
a great bird—a falcon wheeling.

I got a good grip on my desk top, for it seemed to
be a barge drifting down a broad river that could
only be the Nile. Right there on the western bank
rose up the jagged shape of a half-finished pyramid, black against the purple sky. Now the rolling
thunder became the chants and curses of the pyramid builders, dragging stone.

"Imhotep," I said in an unfamiliar language which I seemed to pick up out of the Egyptian air.

"Who?"

The world flooded with electric light, and the schoolroom walls grew up around me again. My desk dropped anchor right where it had been before.

"You, there, that frizzy-headed girl directly behind Alexander Armsworth." Miss Fairweather was calling on me. "Imhotep, did you say?"

It never pays to dispute a teacher. I nodded.

"You seem to be the only one who knows a single fact about Egypt," she remarked. "For it was the wise man Imhotep who was the first great architect of the pyramids. Very good. Who are you?"

"Blossom Culp," I admitted. Letty directed a glance like a dagger in my direction.

"I had about misjudged you, Blossom," Miss Fairweather said generously. "I had thought your mind was wandering."

"Blossom has spells," Letty explained, "and fits. You never know when Blossom is in her right mind and when she isn't. It runs in her family, so I suppose we shouldn't blame her."

"Silence, Letty. If we listened to you, we'd all believe it was the Romans who invented the calendar." Miss Fairweather sneered slightly. "Or the Israelites," she added.

Letty simmered while I preened.

But Miss Fairweather was off and running. "Like all wise peoples," she declared, "the ancient Egyp-

tians prepared themselves for death. How grand
their tombs, fitted out with all the necessities for a
happy afterlife! How perfectly preserved their
mummified bodies! How tightly wrapped the linen
bandages around their scientifically dried loved
ones! How—"

Like the crack of doom a sound split the air. The
cords tied beside the window loosened and
writhed like snakes. With the sound of a rushing
locomotive the window blind began to unfurl.

We've all seen a window blind suddenly fly up,
but who has ever seen one unroll even faster?
Down it roared, depositing Collis Ledbetter with a
thump on the floor, like a small mummified boy
suddenly unwrapped.

We'd all forgotten he was there, and Miss Fairweather had never set eyes on him. The monocle
leapt from her eye, and she grabbed it out of the
air.

She's not the kind of woman who enjoys sur-
prises. "Who might you be?" she inquired, staring
down at him.

His small bootheels were together, and his arms
were crossed on his little chest as they'd been up in
the blind.

"Muffulla Thetfeffer," he said. Then spitting the
handkerchief out of his mouth, he tried again.
"Collis Ledbetter."

Miss Fairweather gaped.

"Would you not be more comfortable at a desk?"
She spoke carefully.

"Oh, I have learned to be comfortable wherever they put me," he said philosophically. "I could hear you fine up there . . . ma'am." Collis pointed a little finger at the top of the window.

This would have been a hard act to follow, but the bell rang. Somehow, we all knew better than to storm out of the place in our French-peasant routine. Miss Fairweather composed her hands before her like we had all the time in the world.

"History is not a sand table," she said in a steady voice. "Nor is it a child's map of flour and water. History is Sink or Swim. And that is what you freshmen will do in this class.

"You will apply your noses to the grindstone. And you will study as you have never studied in all your little lives. Only the diligent will Swim. The Sinkers will be repeating this class next year under my direction."

Her monocle scanned the room and fell again without pity upon Alexander. Once in a while a teacher will pick out an individual student to make an example of for the rest of us. It looked like Alexander had just been appointed to this post. His ears burned like fire, and his narrow shoulders slumped.

"Class dismissed for the time being," Miss Fairweather remarked. The class began to file out, broken in spirit.

Letty hung back, and her spirit was barely bent. She was fighting mad. Drawing out *A Tale of Two Cities* she opened it to her S.T. & B.F.S. meeting agenda. I hung far out to snoop on her, but she was too occupied to notice.

Under Roman Numeral IV, New Business, she filled in as the final item:

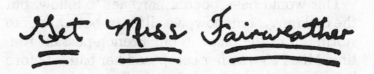

Then she closed the book and gave its cover a confident little pat. I loped off, lost in thought. It looked like Letty was squaring off to bring Miss Fairweather down. I sensed a battle brewing, and it's not my way to sit idle on the sidelines.

3

AFTER THIS BUSY DAY I TOSSED AND TURNED ON my cot through a restless night. It seemed to me that if a person had the choice, it was better to study Egypt under Miss Fairweather than to fall in with Letty. After all, there isn't much to be learned from Letty except how to knuckle under.

It had been Miss Fairweather's interesting lesson that sent me on one of my quick detours into Times Gone By, which made a nice break in the day. I'd glimpsed the old pyramid abuilding and the falcon turning in the ancient sky. I'd felt the green Nile flowing below me, if only for a moment. Give me ancient Egypt in place of freshman year anytime.

Better yet, it looked like I might turn into teacher's pet, as by her own admission Miss Fairweather said I was the only pupil who knew a durn thing about Egypt. As I was making a mental note to bone up on more Egyptian history, I began to drowse and then to sleep and then to dream. It was only the common kind of dream that any ordinary person can have.

Long, mysterious hallways and tunnels are a regular feature of dreams, and this was no exception. I was standing in a passage, very dark and narrow. Because in dreams there's never any going back, I moved forward through curtains of spider web along walls busy with beetles.

And hark! as Miss Blankenship would say. There was light at the end of the tunnel. On I went over stone floors, following this dim gleam growing brighter. Something that didn't bear thinking about slithered over my shoe. Far ahead between me and the light a cat crossed.

When the light expanded, I saw to my horror it was eyes. Two of them poured out flinty blue light, looking right at me. I was pretty sure I was dreaming, for I'm rarely this scared when awake.

These eyes drew me on as the moth to the flame. One eye was enormous and round. The other was hardly more than a slit painted over with a long black line of eye shadow.

Then I thought: Oh, well, those are Miss Fairweather's eyes, and one of them is magnified by the monocle, so I'm surely dreaming. Somewhat encouraged I stepped forth into a small chamber evidently far underground and nowhere near Miss Fairweather's classroom. Now the eyes blinded mine.

They were the eyes of a falcon bird painted with weird artistry on a large box made in a somewhat human form. It stood propped against a wall, and I saw it was solid gold. *Good grief,* my sleeping self said, *whatever next?*

Of course I knew. In this particular dream I'd blundered into an old Egyptian tomb. Then—wouldn't you know it?—The large gold box, clearly a coffin, *moved.*

Just a jiggle at first while I stood within arm's reach, rooted to the spot. This being a dream, the lid of the coffin began to open, its bottom edge scraping the floor.

Trying hard to wake up, I only stood there watching that coffin lid opening by itself, throwing a fearful shadow across my terrified sleeping self.

With an awful clatter the lid on the thing fell away, and I was looking at the ghastly contents: a human form fitted neatly inside.

It was Alexander Armsworth in there, wearing his usual knicker suit and blinking out at me. I knew then for a dead certainty that this was a dream, for Alexander crops up in most of mine. Often he looks better than in real life.

Well, Alexander, I said to him in this dream, *does your mummy know you're out? ha ha.*

But Alexander only blinked.

Cat got your tongue? I inquired.

Never moving from his fitted case, Alexander spoke clearly: *Miss Fairweather said that being the class dunce, I'd have to stand in the corner. For eternity.*

I twitched my elbows, as Letty often does. *Well,*

*Alexander, you're not in a corner. You're in a coffin.
Besides, school's out, and it's the middle of the
night.*

Alexander tried to shake his head. *I believe I'm
stuck, Blossom. I may need a shoehorn to move me.
Give me a hand.* And like a fool, I did. I reached for
Alexander. He reached back. We seemed to em-
brace, this being a dream.

Suddenly he was outside, and I was there in the
coffin where he'd been! He'd pulled a switch on
me, and before I could think, he banged shut the
lid upon my imprisoned form.

Happy Halloween! Alexander called through the
gold lid. Then I heard him scampering off down
the long dark hallway, leaving me to rot.

I soon seemed to use up any leftover air in my
coffin, and the lid began pressing closer upon my
collapsing lungs. I was looking eternity in the face
when the heavy lid turned soft and clinging. And
now my hands were free to fight it. I even got a
mouthful of the thing before I awoke with a start.

Somehow I'd worked in under my old goose-
down pillow, and it was jammed down on my face.
I flung it aside and sat bolt upright in my cot. One
of the panes on my window has been missing these
many years, and I took a gulp of fresh air.

Something had jarred me from my dream. Fearful though it may be, I never cut a dream short
with Alexander in it.

Wan moonlight poured across the sill, drawing
my gaze to the window. Yellow eyes were there,

almond-shaped and gazing back. I shrank. It was a cat, blacker than night, sitting at its ease with its paws wrapped in its tail. It was a perfect stranger to me. Me and Mama don't keep cats because you never know what they're thinking.

I leapt from my cot to scare the thing off, but by the time I got to the window it had vanished with strange speed. Still, I stood at the window with the night air whistling through my old feed-sack nightgown.

This is as good a time as any to explain the circumstances that me and my mama are in. We occupy a two-room shanty on the down side of the streetcar right-of-way. Mama sleeps below on the floor in front of the stove. I sleep above in the attic under the eaves. A ladder leads to my loft through a hole in the floor. Our place of residence is a well-known eyesore, but we're lucky to have it, as we live hand to mouth.

My hand crept to my mouth as I surveyed the scene from my back window. Moonlight struck silver on the naked branches of the cottonwood trees in our grove. Our outhouse stood against the waning moon, and nothing moved for a moment.

Then tree limbs stirred, and a twig snapped beneath a stealthy shoe. Beside the outhouse, branches parted, and an unearthly figure began to edge across the bald yard, scuttling slowly. It was far from human and bent nearly double under a croaker sack thrown over its humped shoulder. It moved nearer, making for our back door.

It was Mama coming home from a busy night's work. There was no telling what was in the heavy pack on her back. As soon as the rest of Bluff City is asleep, she goes into action, and she's out for anything she can get. Leave a single turnip in your garden, and Mama will be all over it. Leave a fish trap or a trout line in the creek, and Mama will land your catch for you. In short, anything that isn't nailed down and some that is, Mama swipes.

Even the city's business district is fair game for her. One time she managed to jimmy loose four of the Civil War cannonballs displayed on the courthouse lawn and tried to pawn them off on the state militia as up-to-date ammunition. There is no stopping Mama.

I heard her shuffling step directly below and her muffled muttering as she eased the croaker sack off her shoulder. Light filtered up through the cracks in the floor when she lit a lamp. Then more mutterings.

I stood by the sill unmoving to hear Mama rip out an oath. "Now where'd you go, you slippery critter?" she said, but evidently not to me.

Chilled through, I turned at last to my cot, lost my way, and gave my chamberpot a resounding kick. It clattered. Before I could make another move, Mama swarmed three rungs up my ladder.

She's not a pretty sight under the best conditions. Now in the ghastly moonlight with her face down at floor level, she looked like a disconnected head that's just rolled away from the guillotine.

The earrings dangling from her ears, while cheap, added to the effect. Her eyes were black smudges under her dark brows, and her hair was a mess.

"Why ain't you in bed, girl? You need every wink of beauty sleep you can git and then some." She grinned without humor. At least she had her teeth in, so she was talking plain. "As long as you're up, come on downstairs and help me look for that thing. Since yore so proud of that Second Sight of yores, or whatever you call it, let's see you make it useful for once."

Mama makes many a bitter joke about my Special Powers, which she says are puny compared to hers. That is as may be. Personally, I think she's faking her powers half the time. Still, you never know with a parent, as they're often smarter than they seem. I followed her down the ladder, giving her no lip, which is the wisest way.

The table where she tells her fortunes and lays out her cards held her haul. It was not one of her better nights: three dry punkins with the frost still on, a handful of black carrots, and the corpse of a young rabbit pried out of a trap. This was all there was you could even think about eating. In a separate, more mysterious heap was a battered stack of cardboard cartons, each labeled POPCORN 5¢, a fake walking stick painted in peeling red, white, and blue with some glitter still stuck on, and a Kewpie doll with but a single weather-beaten feather left to its headdress. Mama had surely been scraping the bottom of some barrel.

"Things is tough all over," she grumbled. "I don't know what the country's coming to."

Still, she didn't seem entirely displeased. Her hooded eyes darted my way. She reached into her shroud and drew out a pouch of Bull Durham. Mama used to buy Bull Durham by the plug and gnaw off enough for a chew. Now she's adopted the more ladylike habit of buying it shredded. Plucking out a dainty pinch she popped it in her jaw.

"I work my fingers to the bone to be a good provider, but it's a losing proposition. I have an idea we're staring the poorhouse in the face."

"Well, Mama," says I, "don't worry about taking charity. You've taken everything else."

"Any more sass like that," she replied, "and you'll be lookin' for yore teeth."

But still she didn't seem too worked up over our plight. Mama's always up to something, and I wondered what. When she thrust the Bull Durham pouch back into her shroud, I heard one of her long thorny fingernails click against some object deep in her pocket. It was hardly a sound at all, but there's nothing wrong with my hearing. Mama froze.

Pretending I'd heard nothing, I said, "Where you been tonight, Mama?"

"Well, I ain't bin to the Daughters of the American Revolution, you can bank on that. Besides, ask no questions, and you'll be told no lies. Jist help me look for somethun that's lost. I had it a minute ago, but now it's gone. It's around here somewheres."

"What is it, Mama?"

"You'll know it when you see it. Feel free to consult that crystal ball if you think it'll help." She chuckled with the sound of dry leaves and was herself beginning to search the room. There was nothing for me to do but follow suit.

She held the lamp in every corner and behind the coal scuttle. Mysteriously, she even climbed up on the chair and searched among the rafters. Though our house is small, it's untidy, and so it took us quite a time.

"I give up," Mama said finally, settling onto the dropped lid of the woodbox. "And you were about as useless as—"

"Well, Mama, I might have seen it and didn't know what it was."

"No, you didn't," she said. "It was a snake."

"A *snake?*"

"That's right. I had him in that poke of mine, thrashin' around. When I reached in for them punkins, out he flowed like water. I had him by the tail, but he turned on me, and I let go. Ain't that a—"

"A *snake?* Why did you bring a snake in here, Mama?"

"Well, I caught him, and it seemed a shame to let him go to waste. It's late in the season for them things, too, so I was lucky." She warmed to her story, crossing one bony knee over the other. "It was real interesting how it happened. I come across this snake over in the pasture by—never mind where. Anyhow, he'd just ate a hedgehog. And when he tried to git away down his hole, he got all jammed up right at that lump in him the hedgehog made!" Mama's lips curled back from her black gums, and she laughed heartily, for her.

"But, Mama," I said hopelessly, "what did you think you were going to do with—him?"

"I thought he'd make a nice pair of shoes, with maybe enough skin left over for a belt." Mama hiked her skirts and glanced down at her present pair of shoes, which don't match.

I sighed. "Mama, I'd just as soon not share the same house with a snake, particularly one big enough to make a pair of shoes, let alone a belt. It could be a copperhead or a water moccasin for all I know."

"Shoot," Mama sneered. "It's nothin' but a common puff adder, and harmless. It's scareder of you than you are of it."

"I doubt that seriously, Mama."

Over my left shoulder I spotted something dangling from the ceiling, swaying. It was an old string of dried garlic onions. I shuddered.

"Well, no use cryin' over spilt milk." Mama smacked her knee. "I expect that puff adder snake snuck out through a hole in the side of the house and is back in the timber by now."

She fingered her pointed chin and tried to look innocent. Both me and Mama knew that snake was not far off, even if it was traveling. But she reached for the old quilt she rolls up in to sleep before the stove. There was nothing for me to do but climb back up to my loft and try to catch forty winks before sunup. But don't think I didn't strip all the covers off my cot and search it from stem to stern before I climbed in.

Then I fell to dreaming again. I was back in Egypt, but at least above ground. In fact I was in the royal palace of Cleopatra, the well-known Egyptian queen. There she sat on her burnished throne wearing a tall crown and a dress that left nothing to the imagination. Cleopatra is the queen who died from being bitten by an asp. Sure enough, the deadly asp was coiled around her arm that very minute and rearing back to strike.

Suddenly Mama popped up in this dream, her ghastly face appearing right behind the throne. "Asp me no questions, and you'll be told no lies," she cackled at me as Cleopatra expired.

I awoke to sunlight, tuckered out.

Shaking out my school clothes with care I dressed and climbed down the ladder to find Mama still flopped before the stove, asleep and snoring. With nothing in sight for breakfast but a rabbit with his fur coat still on and a bunch of black carrots, I was prepared to leave the premises. Then my eye fell on Mama's shroud where she'd left it over a chair.

I moved nearer, keeping one eye on her, though her snores were steady. Just beneath the shroud a narrow twisting form hung to the floor and lay in a small dark puddle of itself. I recoiled. But it was only one of Mama's stockings—black, her favorite color.

I ran a careful hand over her shroud, looking for the pocket. Feeling inside past the Bull Durham pouch my fingers curled over a smooth object. I drew it out.

My eyes popped. In my hand, like a perfect pool of dark blood, was a slick red stone. With one eye still on Mama's form my other eye examined this precious-looking item closer. When I held it up, morning light played through it, throwing another pool of deepest red. Then I saw it was cleverly carved. Only a few markings had been made, but they gave it the shape of an ordinary beetle. A beetle jewel.

I very nearly dropped the thing, which would have been unfortunate. With a trembling hand I worked it back into Mama's shroud and wandered off to school. But I was lost in thought. While small, that beetle jewel was no doubt valuable. With all the trash she'd collected, Mama had evidently hit paydirt. But where? And whose?

4

IT'S NO EASY TASK TO TEACH THE SUBJECT OF history in a town like Bluff City. The students think they already know everything, and the parents are scared they'll learn things they shouldn't. Besides, nobody likes hearing bad news, and history's full of it.

But nothing fazed Miss Fairweather. All on her second day she dragged us through a dozen dynasties of ancient Egypt and threw in the Rosetta Stone for good measure. She was fond of the Rosetta Stone and spoke highly of it.

Then she'd double back on herself and expand upon old King Menes, the first of the pharaohs, or my old pal Imhotep, the pyramid builder, or the invention of some useful item or other, like river barges or money or organized warfare. Those old Egyptians were busy every minute, and so were we. Us freshmen were like a bunch of Israelites led into captivity. And it looked like the Red Sea wasn't going to part and let us out anytime sooner than next spring.

Even when the bell rang, Miss Fairweather looked up annoyed, seeming to think she might throw in one more dynasty. Then she made us wait a full minute before her usual "Class dismissed for the time being."

As we filed out, more dead than alive, her gaze fell on me. "Blossom, approach my desk."

Her monocle studied me as I stood before her, practicing good posture. As usual I'd had no time that morning to do more to my hair than rake my fingers through it. My princess dress from some seasons past is in a sorry state, but I wore over it an old plaid shirt with most of its buttons on.

Thinking perhaps she'd stared too long and seen too much, Miss Fairweather shifted her eyes to my face and cleared her throat.

"As you know, Blossom, every class member is to be responsible for a detailed project on some aspect of ancient Egypt."

How well I knew.

Both her unmatching eyes softened somewhat. "I am expecting great things from your project, Blossom. Just because you may not enjoy certain advantages that the other pupils take for granted, there is no reason why you can't be the brightest spark in the class."

I began to perk up.

"Many great women of history have risen above their disadvantages, Blossom. Even in ancient

Egypt there were women ahead of their time. Take Hat-shep-sut, for but one example."

I was willing.

"Before her, there was not even a word in the Egyptian language for *queen* or *empress*. Did that stop Hat-shep-sut?"

Probably not.

"No, indeed. Through her ambition she ruled the ancient world! Take Tiy, the wife of the Pharaoh Amenhotep the Third. Without a drop of royal blood in her veins she altered the course of history!"

Do tell, I thought.

"Do I make myself clear?" Miss Fairweather inquired. "Even at the dawn of civilization women began their slow rise. Draw your inspiration from them, Blossom, and go forth!" She nodded once to send me forth.

But then she called after me, "And if your path should happen to cross young Master Armsworth's, tell him he had better pull up his socks and apply himself to his studies. Young Alexander needs a careful eye kept on him."

As I couldn't agree more, I continued going forth.

After school I repaired to the library in search of a project topic. When I crept in, the librarian was penned up in a far corner attacking a pile of books with a rubber stamp. Otherwise the school library, being a place of learning, was empty as a tomb. I slunk along toward the stacks.

Attached to these long bookshelves are movable ladders on wheels. As a younger kid I might have taken a joyride on one of them. But since I was looking for inspiration, I decided against horsing around.

Egypt occupied only a few books on a top shelf. It looked like there was room up there for me too. I was soon up a ladder and comfortably stretched out along the leftover end of the shelf. While narrow, it was well lit and warm, with quite a good view over the entire library. Making a pillow out of a pile of pertinent books, I was soon lost in scholarship.

Education is a wonderful thing. In a thick volume called *Ten Years' Digging in Egypt* by the well-known Sir Flinders Petrie I learned that the great scourge of Egypt is grave robbers. Most of the splendors of ancient times have been swiped by these ghouls and sold off at bargain prices. Somebody or other is forever digging in the sands for these precious antiques, and then they flow out of their native land to every corner of the globe.

Come to find out, the pyramids were about useless for hiding the royal mummies themselves. Sooner or later thieves would find the secret passageway to the hidden tomb-room and rob those old mummies blind. "Hardly a tomb has not suffered desecration unspeakable," in the words of Sir Flinders.

As I lay there stretched out and lost in learning, I began to hear a faint scratching somewhere far below me. Mice, I thought, returning to the Land of the Sphinx.

The scratching drew nearer. I peered over the side of my shelf down to the dark and narrow aisle to see a weird crouching figure on the floor, like a crab in a belted jacket.

Squinting, I made out the faint blur of a towheaded boy down there between my bookshelf and another. It was Alexander Armsworth.

The shock of spotting Alexander in a library nearly knocked me off my perch. Speechless, I watched him make his slow way along the floor, painfully on hands and knees. Strange to tell, in his hand was a toothbrush, and he was scouring the floor with it. *What the Sam Hill,* I thought.

Rarely have I ever seen Alexander as busy, working over that floor with a tiny toothbrush. I wondered if the pressures of schoolwork had unhinged his mind. His mind hangs by a single hinge at the best of times.

Directly below he bumped into my ladder and sat back to rest from his labors. In the next moment temptation overcame me. I allowed *Ten Years' Digging in Egypt* to leave my hands, and this heavy book landed directly on Alexander's head.

That took the wind out of his sails, and the toothbrush went skittering. Grabbing his head, he looked up to see if the sky was falling and saw me instead.

"Dad-burn it, Blossom Culp. If you're not behind me, you're above me, dropping lead weights," he whined. "Besides, what are you doing up there stretched out on the shelf like a corpse in the morgue? That's no way to use a library."

"I guess I'm not familiar with library routine," I answered. "I didn't even think to bring a toothbrush." I grinned. Alexander didn't.

"There's much to be learned up here on the top shelf, Alexander," I pointed out. "We of the twentieth century are one lucky people. All this interesting lore of ancient times is an open book to us. Before they dug up that Rosetta Stone here a while back, nobody could crack the code of all the old writings, which were known as hieroglyphics and pictograms. Without that Rosetta Stone to explain everything, it would all be Greek to us."

"Lay off," said Alexander. "It's all the Rosetta Stone's fault. Otherwise we wouldn't have to study Egypt. That lump of rock is a millstone around my neck."

"It better be a grindstone to keep your nose to," I said. "And if you're not in the library to do a project for Miss Fairweather, what do you think you're doing here?"

Alexander grew shifty and retrieved his toothbrush. "Private business," he muttered.

"But in a public place," I reminded him.

"Iota Nu Beta," mumbled Alexander mysteriously.

"I ought to know better?" I echoed. "How true."

"Naw," he said. "Iota Nu Beta. It's the high-

school fraternity. Blossom, you wouldn't even
know what a fraternity is."

"A criminal gang?" I offered.

"It's an exclusive club of sophomores, juniors,
and seniors themselves with a strictly secret membership."

"Don't tell me you've fallen in with an older
bunch again, Alexander. You know the sorry
messes you've gotten yourself into with those two
big galoots Bub Timmons and Champ Ferguson."

Alexander sniffed. "Iota Nu Beta takes in a
higher-type boy and is completely organized, with
a constitution and a secret handshake. They honor
as pledges but few freshman boys, and I have been
chosen."

I pondered this senseless turn of events. "And
where does the toothbrush come in?" I pried.

Alexander gazed at its filthy bristles. "It's part of
the initiation. A fraternity pledge such as myself
has to scrub down most of the school to prove himself worthy of full membership." He glanced down
the aisle furtively. "They check up on me once in a
while."

Few things amaze me, but this did. "Alexander,
what if your mama made you scrub the floors of
your own house even with a full-size brush?"

He looked up, struck dumb with horror at the
thought.

"Let me get this straight," I said. "If you scrub
down half of Bluff City, then the Iota Nu Betas will

show you their handshake and tell you their
secrets?" It seemed a poor bargain to me.

"There's more to it than that," he mumbled,
glancing again over his shoulder. "They say this is
the easy part."

As it happened, I could monitor the entire library from my high perch on the top shelf. I
glanced up by chance to see Letty Shambaugh tee-
tering on the doorsill. She's no more a regular user
of the library than Alexander. But there she was,
her little lips pursed, her little eyes roaming
around this unfamiliar territory. She was looking
for something, and it wasn't knowledge. It was Alexander, because it always is.

"Scoot that ladder my way," I told him. "I'd better be checking out these books if I want to keep
Miss Fairweather happy." As I descended the ladder with an armload of books, I added, "If you take
my advice, Alexander, you'll apply yourself to a
project of your own if you don't want to end up a
Sinker."

"I have my social standing to consider," he muttered. "It takes up a lot of my time."

I'd come to the bottom rung and was all but in
the arms of Alexander, who was steadying the ladder. Then I was inspired. My foot slipped, and my
books went everywhere. I pitched off the ladder,
and Alexander caught me.

"Whoops," I said softly, clinging to him.

At that very moment Letty Shambaugh appeared at the end of our aisle, right on cue. I clung

to Alexander an extra moment before thrusting him aside with a small flourish.

"Oh, Alexander!" says I in a dainty voice. He caught sight of Letty and staggered back a second too late.

"Well, if that doesn't about take the cake!" Letty barked, planting her little fists on her hips.

I turned in astonishment to see her there. She spun on her little heel and flounced off, deeply disgusted.

I got Alexander to walk me home by promising to square him with Letty. Though in my opinion he's not as sweet on her as she is on him, he's about half trapped in her web and fears her sting. Besides, if word reached the general public that me and him had been spooning in the library stacks, it would do his social standing no good.

"But will Letty believe we met in there purely by accident?" He made a fist and pounded his forehead.

"If I speak slow and simple enough, she may be able to grasp it." I smiled at the picture of me ever bothering to explain anything to Letty. "But if you're all tied up being a pledge of the Iota Nu Betas, Alexander, you'll have no time for the likes of Letty.

"As for Miss Fairweather," I added, "when she hears you have no time for history, I wouldn't care to think what steps she'll take. I hope nobody tells her."

He flinched, but his mind was elsewhere. "All I need from you, Blossom, is to square me with Letty, and I'll be much obliged."

"Anything to oblige, Alexander," I said to his retreating form.

I stood on a streetcar tie as dusk descended over Bluff City and swallowed up Alexander. By and large I wasn't displeased with the day now drawing to a close. Both Letty and Alexander were as jumpy as a couple of cats in a room full of rocking chairs. I don't take much pleasure in the discomfort of others. But I take some.

Turning, I saw a wisp of smoke rising out of our chimney along with a combination of smells, some good, some not so good. Mama was cooking one of our rare suppers.

As it turned out, we had two kinds of pie, rabbit and punkin, with a side order of carrots. And as Mama always says, "Hunger is the best sauce." While she demolished a plate of vittles, I watched her across the table. Though her manners are bad, she was eating her head off with innocent pleasure as if such things as snakes and precious stones carved like beetles weren't within miles of us.

You would need your own personal Rosetta Stone to decipher the peculiar ways of a parent.

5

ON THE FOLLOWING MORNING IN ENGLISH
class a small piece of folded paper lit on my desk.
As I say, nobody ever passes a note to me, and this
one came from Letty's direction, which was
stranger still.

Thinking her aim was bad, I picked up this note
with only my fingertips and tried to return it. But
she made an impatient clucking sound in her
throat.

"It's for *you*. Read the thing and stop waving it
around."

Puzzled, I unfolded the note to read in Letty's
scrawl the following:

```
Blossom:
    The Sunny Thoughts and Busy Fingers
Sisterhood is holding its November meet-
ing at my house this afternoon at
4 o'clock. You are invited to attend
as an interested outsider for this
meeting and this meeting only.
    Promptness is vital as my agenda is
long. Be there.
                Letty Shambaugh, President
```

This piece of literature took my mind completely off *A Tale of Two Cities*. But I smelled a rat. When the bell rang and we'd all stampeded out to the hall, I took the bull by the horns.

Being seen talking to me in public is not Letty's favorite thing, but I blocked her path. "Say, listen," says I, "let's cut the cackle and get down to brass tacks. What do you want me for at your so-called meeting? You want something."

Mincing words gets you nowhere with Letty. Her eyes darted from side to side while she hoped to be saved by one of her sisterhood. Giving up on that, she plastered her prettiest expression all over her face.

"Well, Blossom, you were *such* a help to the entire freshman class during our recent Halloween Haunted House, I just naturally thought of you as we prepare for the annual Homecoming Parade. Mercy, I don't know what we'd do without all your interesting ideas."

"Try again, Letty."

Her little smile drooped, and her eyes went slightly out of focus. We were nose to nose, and any minute now some member of the general public was going to start wondering why.

Her expression toughened somewhat. "Since you're such a *prize pupil* of Miss Fairweather's," she snapped, "I thought you might give us all some pointers about how to get along with her."

"Get along with her or get the goods on her?" I inquired.

Letty's eyes shifted to shifty. We were getting nearer the truth, never a short trip.

"And what else?" I said.

She studied me a moment while her tiny tongue darted snakily out from the corner of her mouth. "To be frank, Blossom, I'd just as soon have you in my sight. It is entirely for your own good. I do not want to see you getting your hopes up regarding Alexander. I have always said that you have your feelings almost like anybody else. And I for one would not like to see you heartbroken. The truth is that as soon as Alexander is initiated into Iota Nu Beta, he is going to pin me."

"What's he going to do to you?" I said, quite shaken up.

Letty's throat clucked again. "He is going to give me his fraternity pin, and I will wear it here." She pointed to the left side of one of the ruffles on her starchy blouse. "It is a seed pearl."

"What is?" I peered closer at the left side of her chest.

"The fraternity pin, of course."

"And what's getting pinned to Alexander supposed to mean?"

Letty sketched an airy little gesture in the air. "Oh, it means we're engaged to be engaged—something like that. Nothing to concern you, Blossom."

"So you want me at your meeting to keep me out of Alexander's vicinity and to watch you gloat over bagging him," I said. "Is that about the size of it, Letty?"

"Blossom," she said down her nose, "true sisterly friendship is lost on you."

Then as we were both in deadly danger of being late to history, we cut and run.

Since I wouldn't have missed it for the world, I found myself mounting Letty Shambaugh's porch at the stroke of four P.M. I was alone because the S.T. & B.F.S. girls had run a foot race all the way from school behind their president to keep from walking with me.

If you'd been boning up on the old Egyptians like I had, you'd know they crammed their tombs with everything a person could possibly need in the Afterlife: fine furniture and fancy togs, good dishes and actual food, alabaster urns and realistic statues. All quality merchandise.

This is much the way the Shambaughs are set up for this life. Their residence is a well-known brick landmark on Fairview Avenue. There's much plate glass in the front door, and on either side are large bay windows heaped full of ferns. Inside, the place is jammed to the rafters with priceless antiques, as Mrs. Shambaugh is a famous collector. Before I could ring the electric bell, the door fell open to reveal her tremendous form.

"My stars! Blossom!" she said, stepping back.

If Letty's worried about where to find her figure, she should apply to her mama, who has enough for two. Mrs. Shambaugh has an upper deck on her like the *Titanic*.

When she recovered from the shock of me on

her doorstep, she swept me inside. "How thought-
ful of Letty to include you in her little club meeting, Blossom," she boomed. "I have always said
that Letty is too generous for her own g— I mean
to say, how pleased they will all be to see you!"

Somewhat distracted, Mrs. Shambaugh dragged
me into her antique-crammed front hall. "The girls
are holding their little meeting in that room behind the stairs where Mr. Shambaugh smokes his
nightly cigar. Scoot along down there, Blossom."
She planted a hand in the small of my back to start
me off.

I scooted along over the deep carpet and soon
entered the sacred sanctuary of the S.T. & B.F.S.,
which killed their conversation dead. The gang
was all there: Ione and Nola and Harriet and big
Maisie Markham and the Beasley twins, Tess and
Bess, who are identical. When I joined their midst,
they all looked to Letty for guidance.

"There you are, Blossom." She ran a hand
through her golden curls. "Better late than never."

"Never," Maisie Markham echoed.

I started to settle in their circle on the floor between Tess and Bess, but they can't be separated.
So I wedged in between Nola and Ione. Letty stood
in her position as president, taking the floor.

"Shut up, girls," she began, "because I call this
meeting to order. The first regular item on the
agenda is Grooming Tips and Beauty Secrets. But
as we have a full program, we'll have to give that a
lick and a promise. Does anyone have any progress

to report since our last meeting regarding bust size?"

Everyone looked down to inspect her own chest, or just plain hung her head. Even I took a gander at mine, since there's nothing greater than the power of suggestion.

"If not," said Letty, "we come to Roman numeral II on my agenda. This is refreshments and a surprise treat. And since Mother won't leave us in peace until she gets her refreshments served, we'll have them now. Come in, Mother!" she bawled. "I know you're hiding outside the door!"

It burst open, and Mrs. Shambaugh sailed in. When she swooped down to rest a heavy tray of eats on the floor, her pearls swayed far out from her mammoth upper deck, putting us all to shame. "And there is plenty more where that came from, girls!" she thundered. Meaning the refreshments.

"Just call out if you need anything. I am never far away."

"Too true," Letty said behind clenched teeth.

When Mrs. Shambaugh departed, leaving the door slightly ajar, we fell on the food. It was a plate of finger sandwiches heaped on a bed of parsley to be chased by small glasses of apple juice. Maisie Markham ate with both hands, but Mrs. Shambaugh had allowed for this. I ate my share too. The crusts were all trimmed from the bread, so you needed several.

We ate our fill, and everybody chattered to everybody else but me. But I hadn't come to this particular event unprepared. I always believe in making a contribution when you're an invited guest.

Since nobody was paying any attention to me anyhow, they didn't see me reach into the pocket of my shirt and draw out a worm. As I say, we were still cutting up worms in the biology class, and I'd saved a whole one back for a special occasion. Though dead, he was in fine condition: one of those fleshy white ones with pink at both ends and about six inches long.

Seeming to reach for another finger sandwich, I palmed my worm bent double and popped him under the lid of one of the lower sandwiches. For good measure I poked in a sprig of parsley. I got away with it, too, and sat back to let nature take its course. It's said that eating a worm won't kill you, so my conscience was clear.

Bye and bye Letty got up and switched off the light of one of her mama's antique alabaster lamps. Then she drifted over to pull the velvet curtains across the window, dimming the room. Sweeping up a large object off her paw's desk, she came back to stand over us dramatically.

"Now, girls, here comes the surprise treat on the program. It's a new talent of mine I've been practicing on the sly!"

She smiled fondly at herself and plonked a square wooden thing down in the middle of our circle. A finger sandwich nearly lodged in my throat when I saw it was a Ouija board.

"Good heavens, what is that thing?" said several, staring down at all the letters, numbers, and mystic symbols printed on it. Of course I knew. A Ouija board is a method for making contact with the Spirit World. It's even been known to work when used by experienced hands, which Letty's aren't.

On the board she placed a little arrow-shaped piece of wood. This device, known as a planchette, will move from letter to letter, spelling out telepathic messages, often from the dead. But such messages are easily faked and downright dangerous in the wrong hands, which Letty's are.

Right then and there I decided it was time to call it a day. Edging back, I spoke up. "Well, I'd better be on my way," I said. "I am a Psychic Sensitive and you won't catch me hanging around the vicinity of a Ouija board in the hands of amateurs." I meant it too. "Ouija boards are tricky things, and I know my limits, unlike certain people," I added to make my position clear.

The rest of them would have let me go gladly, but Letty said, "Sit down and shut up, Blossom. You have bragged near and far about your so-called Second Sight and all the many witches flying around your family tree until we are up to here with it. Now when you learn that I, too, have a Spiritualist Gift, you are pea-green with envy."

"Positively pea-green," said Maisie Markham on cue while I simmered.

Much as I dreaded that Ouija board stretched out before us, my pride was involved. The day I find myself envious of Letty Shambaugh, I'll drink Lysol. I wondered if calling her bluff would do me any good.

Tucking up my knees I said, "First off you can receive no messages on that thing without making contact through a Control, which is a—"

"I am perfectly familiar with Controls as well as everything else." Letty twitched her elbows importantly. "I have already made contact with one on the Other Side. My Control is a girl who has been dead for one hundred and twenty-five years by the name of Phoebe. She met her tragic end in the . . . er . . . French Revolution."

Several of us gasped in wonder, though not me.

"Phoebe was an aristocrat of good family, so the two of us have a lot in common."

"Bound to," said Maisie on cue while I pondered.

"Here, girls, I'll show you how it works." Letty flopped down on the floor and planted a heavy finger on the planchette.

You're only supposed to rest your fingertips lightly on the planchette and let it move over the board as it sees fit. But Letty left nothing to chance. She bore down on that planchette like she was driving nails.

Silence descended. "Is anyone there?" she asked in a so-called ghostly voice.

But the public is easily fooled. Already, Ione was grabbing one of my arms and Nola the other. The planchette skidded off, guided by Letty's urgent fingers. It raced straight to three letters: Y E S.

"Whoooo is out there in the Great Beyond?" she moaned.

Some of us watched spellbound while the planchette lumbered heavily to six letters: F E E B E E.

Trust Letty not even to know the right spelling for *Phoebe*.

I began to relax a little. If this was as close as we were going to get to the Spirit World, this room was the safest place in Bluff City.

"Are you happy where you are, dear departed Phoebe, after your dreadful death in the . . . er . . . French Revolution?"

Y E S.

"How happy can she be, without a head?" I remarked, but Nola dug me hard in the ribs.

"Have you a message for one of us here in the Land of the Living?" Letty called out. "And if so, who?"

Y O U

"Oh, lucky you," Maisie said, banging Letty on the back.

"And what have I got coming to me, Phoebe?" Letty wondered. For two cents I'd have told her myself.

A G I F T

"Oh, goody." Letty bounced and leaned on the planchette with the heel of her hand. "What is it?"

I N B

Everybody stared, deciphering these three letters. Then they all fell back squealing. Iota Nu Beta, of course.

Letty squealed loudest. "Well, girls, now that Phoebe has let the cat out of the bag, you may as well know that as soon as Alexander Armsworth is initiated into Iota Nu Beta, I will be the proud wearer of his fraternity pin. The Spirits are never wrong!"

She was flushed with triumph, having put across the announcement she'd meant to make. But nothing is ever enough for Letty. Her eyes fell on me and narrowed. "Well, Blossom, top that!"

Everybody sat there gloating. They all knew the doggone Ouija board worried me. Worse yet, Letty had been tempting fate by making light of it. I was jumpier than turtle parts in a pan and playing for time. Then the unexplainable happened.

The planchette Letty had been holding jumped out of her hand, arched over the Ouija board, and fell in my lap. Nobody quite saw that but me and her. To the others it looked like she'd tossed it to me. She hadn't. Letty swallowed a gasp while my eyes popped.

Gingerly, I placed the planchette on the worrisome board. Forgetting to place my fingertips on it in the prescribed manner, I drew back.

It moved. Just a whisker at first. Then its pointed end turned first one way and then the other, seemingly confused.

With all my might I tried to make my mind a clean slate empty of all thought. It was a struggle, because I'd been cramming my head full of Egyptian learning from the library books.

But it looked like matters were beyond my control. Like a small dog just let off its leash, the planchette began nosing among letters, feeling its way. My hands lay useless in my lap, and my brain burned.

"How does Blossom do that?" asked Ione, wondering at the automatic planchette.

"Powers of concentration," I lied, still trying to keep my mind a blank.

The planchette moved with more confidence, pointing to various letters:

H A T H O R

When it reached the last letter and rested, the heavy curtains at the window stirred slightly. Out of a probably clear sky I heard thunder and hoped to keep it distant.

Believe me, for a moment the Sisterhood and I were not in the room by ourselves. Something or someone invisible was there. I thought I heard the tinkling bells of light laughter, and it was far from Letty's screechy giggle.

The scent of some rare perfume wafted through the room: a whiff of incense and cedar. Several of the girls put up their noses and sniffed at this pleasant aroma. But Letty only stared at me horrified. I fought with all my might against some force among us.

As I say, these Ouija boards can run riot on you. I blinked repeatedly to keep my eyeballs from rolling back. Then we all heard the sound of a small piece of wood splintering. The planchette cracked in two and lay broken on the Ouija board. We all stared and held our breaths.

"I guess Blossom concentrated too hard," Harriet said, casting me a halfway respectful glance which Letty intercepted. Without trying, I'd shown her up. Because of me that planchette had run rings around her dreamed-up Phoebe and then turned itself into matchsticks.

Taking over again, Letty screeched a high laugh. "Oh, well, what does HATHOR mean, anyhow? If it is a word at all, it's misspelled."

Now, that really got my goat. I'm a champion speller, and if you don't believe it, just check over this page.

"As I have always said," Letty went on, "the Ouija board is more of a parlor game than anything else. I believe it runs on the principle of perpetual motion or electric currents in the air or some such thing."

With considerable presence of mind she swept up the board and the remains of the planchette and tossed them aside. She was just reaching for her agenda when the sound of an electric bell electrified the room. Already edgy, everybody screamed and grabbed everybody else, me included.

It was the telephone ringing out in the hall. Being well connected the Shambaughs are also connected to the telephone company. Because she's never far away, Mrs. Shambaugh lifted the receiver and bellowed, *"Hello Shambaugh residence Mrs. Shambaugh speaking."* She scarcely needs this instrument to be heard all over town.

"Speak up," she roared. *"There is static on the line. What? Certainly not. I am not trying to call Cairo. What? Besides, I do not know a soul in Cairo. Hello? Hello?"*

We sat in a silent circle while Mrs. Shambaugh

banged the receiver back on the hook and muttered loud to herself, "I have always said that apparatus is more trouble than it's worth. Cairo, Illinois, indeed, as if I would know anybody in that godforsaken burg."

She stalked off down the hall while the Sisterhood girls nudged one another and tittered. But my thoughts were troubled. A botched-up telephone connection to Cairo, Illinois, was doubtless a mere brainwave of mine picked up and misread by the Ouija board going haywire. I'd known right along that Letty's heavy hand on that thing could only spell trouble. In fact, that's about all she can spell.

Then, as I stared fixedly out the window in the direction of the setting sun, I saw a large beetle climbing the outside of the pane, black against the blood-red sunset. The beetle scuttled and paused and scuttled again. It looked to me like it was trying to get in. Mere bug though it was, it bothered me. And it recalled a certain beetle-shaped jewel I'd held in my trembling hand.

There were signs and portents everywhere. I shuddered.

6

IF IT WAS THE DAY OF JUDGMENT, LETTY would still work through her entire agenda. I've always marveled at how she can keep that Sisterhood of hers under her thumb. She soon had them where she wanted them again, eating out of her hand and agreeing to anything as if that whole planchette business had never happened.

They swept over Roman numeral III, Old Business. It was to be nothing but a general pooling of ignorance on the subject of boys anyway.

"And now," Letty announced, "we come to New Business, which is the important part of my agenda.

"It is our Sisterhood's duty to take the lead in coming up with a prime idea for a float to represent the freshman class in this year's Homecoming Parade. Nobody at the high school ever expects much from a freshman float, and so, girls, our honor is at stake. In the Homecoming Game our team is playing their old rivals, the Bloomington Bulldogs, and so after giving it my deep consideration I have decided that the theme of our float will be "Put the Bulldogs in the Doghouse."

"Brilliant," said Maisie Markham, and everybody agreed.

And then if they didn't all divide up into committees regarding such weighty matters as crêpe paper and chicken wire and all the fixings for a float in the shape of a doghouse. The idea of dragging such a monstrosity as this thing promised to be through all the streets of Bluff City before a football game left me cold. But at least it was a safer topic than you-know-what.

With Letty holding us to her agenda we came at last to the final item of New Business. It involved Miss Fairweather.

"Now, girls," Letty said, drawing them into their tightest circle, "I am sure we are all agreed that something must be done about Miss Fairweather. If we do not take steps, she is going to ride roughshod all over us. If we bow to all her demands about studying Egypt until our brains fall out, there will be no time whatever for the more important issue of Homecoming."

They all nodded and pulled their mouths into determined level lines.

"Miss Fairweather waltzes in here in the middle of the semester and starts laying down the law. And I ask you, girls, by what right? And why was a so-called qualified schoolteacher *available* at this time of year?"

None of us had wondered about that, including me. Letty had us right where she wanted us.

"I will tell you why we are *honored* by Miss Fairweather's presence. And I have it on the best authority. Every respectable woman in town knows, because it is all over the Daughters of the American Revolution. Miss Fairweather was *fired* from her last teaching position at Peoria Central High School!"

Letty preened while this bombshell broke over us.

Then she glared at Maisie, who remembered to say, "Fired! Whatever for?"

"I'm glad you asked." Letty lowered her voice. "It turned out she was a . . . suffragette."

"Oh, my stars," Maisie cried, covering her ears. "Don't tell me."

"What's a suffragette?" asked Tess or Bess.

Letty gladly explained. It's a person who believes that women should be allowed to vote on Election Day, the same as men. As I understand it, they're called suffragettes because they're made to suffer for their beliefs.

"I, for one," said Letty, "certainly have no use for the vote. Voting is unwomanly, and if you ask me, Miss Fairweather is a dangerous agitator. We have run one history teacher out of town, and we can do it again. This whole suffragette movement

could start spreading and become a threat to the
community!"

"How true!" bellowed Mrs. Shambaugh. Except
for when the telephone got its wires crossed, she'd
spent the whole afternoon wedged behind the
door eavesdropping on us. Now she burst in again
with her sails full of wind and dropped anchor.

"Attend to Letty!" Mrs. Shambaugh hollered at
us, her pearls whipping around. "No real woman
wants to sashay down to the polls and cast her vote.
It is only a place where men hang out using bad
language and spittoons because on Election Day
the saloons are closed by law. Girls, I would sooner
set foot in a saloon myself or a billiard parlor before
I'd be caught dead in a polling place!"

She paused for breath. "As I often tell Letty, it is
a woman's destiny to convince her husband to vote
the way she sees fit. Women were put on this earth
to tell men what to do. I, for one, send off Mr.
Shambaugh to the voting booth completely easy in
my mind!"

As I say, the Day of Judgment wouldn't break up
one of Letty's meetings early, but something else
did. In the midst of her tirade Mrs. Shambaugh
chanced to look down into Maisie Markham's big
round face.

Throughout the proceedings Maisie had been
feeding steadily from the plate of finger sandwiches. Now she came to the last one and was
beginning to wolf away at it.

Mrs. Shambaugh went deathly pale when she

saw one half of a biology specimen depending from Maisie's gnawing jaw.

"Saints in heaven, Maisie! What in creation is that thing dangling out of your mouth? Stop chewing at once, and I forbid you to swallow!"

These loud words naturally caused the entire sisterhood to look Maisie's way. I personally didn't look because I knew it wouldn't be a pretty sight.

Pierced with screams, the meeting broke up early amid much gagging and heaving. I crept away for home unnoticed. It's not my way to overstay my welcome. All in all it was just as well, for I was to have ahead of me the busiest night of my life to date.

It was no sooner night than Mama sent me out into it. Not content to plunder most of Bluff City herself, she often packs me off on some dark mission. I don't even care to recall how many times I've been shot at in henhouses or chased with rakes out of garden patches.

This seemed to be another such night. Mama handed me a paring knife to put in one of my shoe tops and a candle and matches for the other. Then she thrust a folded-up croaker sack at me and pointed a crooked finger to the door.

As missions for Mama go, this was not one of the worst. I was to spend the nighttime hours digging up the root of the sassafras tree. This particular root brews up into a medicinal tea. Mama drinks it herself and sells the root with certain promises as a miracle cure. Happily, these sassafras trees are found in outlying parts where I can usually work without interference. Off I went, making my way by moonlight to the nearest timber.

As luck would have it, my route led me along the streetcar tracks past the property of Old Man Leverette. Because I've tangled with this stout old party before, I had every intention of breezing right by his place.

He's a retired farmer moved to town, and as he lives on the same side of the tracks as me and Mama, his property is far from modern. At the end of his punkin patch stands an outdoor privy. I was practically past it when I heard muffled laughter rising from the far side of Old Man Leverette's compost heap between me and the privy. I slowed my pace.

When a cloud had cleared the moon, I saw the heads of a group of boys. They were snuffling and whispering loudly, as boys will. I paused.

Considering it my duty as a good neighbor to Old Man Leverette, I swerved off the streetcar tracks and made my way up to his compost heap. Glancing toward the house I saw not a light showing from it, as this old farmer retires early. Drawn on by my duty to this property owner I climbed the compost heap unnoticed by the group hunkered on the far side. They were smoking, of course. By the light of their glowing butts I made out the faces of Wendell Burdick, Monroe Puckett, and Orville Tweedy from the high school. There were two or three others I couldn't put a name to, all older than us freshmen. Typical of boys in a bunch they thought they were alone in the world.

"Haw, haw," they said, jostling one another where they squatted, "he ought to be green as a gourd by now. Or cured like a ham, haw haw." One and all kept glancing toward the side of Old Man Leverette's privy, and I wondered what the Sam Hill was going on.

From the privy itself wisps of smoke rose through a knothole and drifted across the moon, even though this well-built structure is tight against the weather. *What devilment is this?* I asked myself. But the mystery began to clear. With a wave of his hand Wendell Burdick sent Orville Tweedy around to the front of the outhouse.

Speaking directly at the door Orville said, "Say, in there, pledge-brother Armsworth, are you still breathing?"

"Barely," came a stifled voice within.

In surprise my knee slipped and planted itself in slimy compost. This crowd had Alexander cooped up in Old Man Leverette's privy! Then I knew they were the so-called secret fraternity of Iota Nu Beta. Alexander was still being initiated. I was all ears to hear more.

"Oh, lowly pledge Armsworth, how far down have you smoked that seegar?" Orville wafted around his cigarette in the open air and hitched a thumb in the top of his knickers. We waited awhile for Alexander's answer.

"About half," he moaned faintly, "as near as I can tell." Then he was seized by a fit of coughing.

The squatting Iota Nu Betas were seized by a fit of chortling and pounded each other's back.

"Not quite half, by our calculations," Orville said through the door. "Remember the rule, oh, lowly pledge. Don't quit puffing on that stogie until it's burned down to your unworthy fingers. We can wait, and we've got all night. Do we make ourselves clear?"

". . . Clear . . ." said the fading Alexander from within his narrow smokehouse.

As soon as Orville rejoined them, all the Iota Nu Betas were climbing to their feet. Without a murmur they began to file stealthily away past the stand of dry hollyhocks and off the property. You wouldn't believe how quiet this bumbling bunch could move when they put their minds to it. As quick as they were gone, there wasn't a sign of human life anywhere except for the wispy smoke curling from the privy.

If this didn't about take the cake, as Letty would say. There Alexander was all alone and smoking like a chimney. While he thought the Iota Nu Betas were standing guard on him, they'd shortly all be home snug in their beds. Easing down off the compost I began to wonder how I might improve on this tailor-made situation.

Rounding the heap I shuffled my feet in the fallen leaves to make the sound of several boys still present. Then I strolled to the front of the privy.

Carved in the door was a half-moon shape that provided the only ventilation. This opening had been stuffed full of corn shocks to block it up. I'll say this for the Iota Nu Betas: they're thorough.

Glancing down I saw the door wasn't even latched. Alexander could have walked out a free man if he'd dared. For a moment I considered locking the door. Why not let him cure in there like a ham till daybreak? It might cure him of both cigars and fraternities, if it didn't smother him.

Then, come dawn, when Old Man Leverette paid a necessary morning call on his own outhouse, there Alexander would be, cluttering up his private property, green as a gourd and sick as a horse. I pictured Old Man Leverette's outrage at this discovery and wondered if it would be outrage enough.

Possibly not, I thought, as I recalled the case against Alexander. For one thing he was wasting valuable time on this fraternity tomfoolery. For another, he was putty in Letty's hands and would pin her the first chance he got.

The more I considered it, the more polecat Alexander appeared. I searched my mind for a punishment to fit his crimes. In the meantime I cleared my throat and cast my voice as deep as Orville Tweedy's, which is none too deep.

Rapping sharply on the privy door I growled, "Lowlife pledge Armsworth, how far down have you smoked that-there seegar?"

". . . A long way . . ," said Alexander distantly, ". . . too far. . . ."

"Keep a-puffing," I said Orvillishly.

From within came small sucking sounds interrupted by gagging. Then I was struck by a pair of inspirations. "Say, listen, worthless pledge Armsworth," I said, "the next part of your initiation will take place at school tomorrow—early. Make that no later than homeroom."

Smoky silence from within as Alexander waited for his fate.

"You know that little frizzy-headed girl that sits behind you?"

"Blah," came Alexander's voice, "Blossom."

"That's her," said the Orville person. "Tomorrow, no later than homeroom, you're to kiss Blossom. In public."

The privy stood stunned into silence.

"Be sure you do it, too, because our spies are everywhere." To be on the safe side I added, "And don't expect to be told again."

"Aargh," Alexander said from within, no doubt because the stogie was getting to him.

Then I moved on to my second inspiration. Why lock Alexander in till morning to be found? Why not work out a way of bringing Old Man Leverette's attention to this matter right now while I was here to witness? I went to work at once, recalling that many of my best ideas are spur of the moment.

Bending to my chore I gathered up several armloads of dry leaves and made a nice pile of them in a little clearing between the compost heap and the privy itself.

A cheery little bonfire here would do Old Man Leverette a favor in cleaning up his property. Moreover, its light might just rouse him from his slumbers. I'd have burned down his compost heap, which was handy, but it was far too slimy to give a nice glow. Pulling out a box of matches from my shoe top I set my bonfire ablaze. A dab of coal oil would have come in useful, but I did the best with what I had.

Then I withdrew to a far corner of the yard behind the hollyhocks. From there I had a clear view of the entire Leverette place from the privy up to the back of the house. A small sunrise appeared to break over the vicinity as my bonfire took hold and began to burn. Shortly, the rear windows of the Leverette residence began to reflect orange flame.

It was right about then that my plan got out of hand. A sudden gust of night breeze swept over the bonfire, and a clutch of burning leaves spiraled upward like a torch in an invisible hand. This floating fireball breezed over to the outhouse roof and snagged on the tarpaper. In a twinkling the entire top of the privy lit up like a Christmas tree before my horrified eyes. It licked high into the bare tree branches, showering sparks.

"Fire!" I called out, practicing good citizenship.

The privy spoke suddenly in Alexander's voice. "Yeow!" he screeched. "I am being fried alive!"

Then came the terrible sound of Alexander flinging himself against every wall except the door. He
was also whooping like a crane. Alerted at last, Old
Man Leverette exploded through his screen door
and came pounding off the porch and down the
punkin patch. His old nightshirt switched around
his big, thrashing legs. With his white mane of hair
and his lion's face bright red with exertion and
reflected flame, he was a sight.

"Far! *Far!*" he hollered in his countrified accent.

A hook and ladder company couldn't have saved
the outhouse by then, but onward Old Man Leverette galloped. Alexander found the unlatched
privy door and rocketed out, head down and
elbows pumping. At his top speed he butted Old
Man Leverette square in the middle of the nightshirt.

Even above the crackling of the fire you could
hear the sound of the air going out of the old gentleman. He and Alexander staggered apart. Alexander was wobbly on his pins anyhow, and in his
haste still clung to a good-sized cigar, which he
held high like a riverboat gambling man.

Though his property was afire and the air was
knocked out of him, Old Man Leverette made a
lunge for Alexander. What with the butting and
the flying tackle it was a better show than the high-
school football team puts on. Alexander made a
skittering skip backward, and Old Man Leverette
grabbed air. Like a bat Alexander streaked off into

the night, though of course smoking is not good for your wind.

"Smokin' in my privy!" Old Man Leverette howled, shaking both fists after Alexander. *"Just wait, buster. I seen you. I'll know you again."*

But I doubted it. I'd have hardly known Alexander myself, for he was green as a gourd.

The flaming door of the privy fell forward in a spurt of sparks, and the walls had burned down to the level of the seat and were flickering out. The entire vicinity smelled fierce. Old Man Leverette stood with his heavy fists on his tremendous hips, using the kind of language men use in saloons and polling places. Finding no comfort he kicked at the ground with a bare foot and stomped back to his house.

I waited till the coast was clear, and then I went about my business. But before I left the property, I searched around on the ground to find the cigar Alexander had flung away. Knocking off its warm ash I popped it into my sassafras sack. Then I lit out for the tall timber.

7

IT WAS NEARLY DAWN BEFORE I'D DUG ENOUGH sassafras root to satisfy Mama. I'm not nervous of night, as you're always safest when your fellow humans are asleep. But it was eerie when the moon began to climb down the sky. All the way home from the timber I had as companion a large night-bird swooping above me, whirring in the air. It was the size of a chickenhawk or some such a thing. When it wasn't behind me, it drifted ahead on the night breeze, following and then leading me. I thought little about it, but some.

At home I left the sack of sassafras where Mama couldn't miss it when she came in from her own nocturnal chores. Then I climbed up to the attic for an hour or two of well-earned sleep. After shaking out all my bedclothes, as was my new habit, I soon fell into my cot and began sawing logs.

Something stirred me a while after. It wasn't a sound, though I smelled the scent of cedar and incense. Imagine my horror when I opened my eyes, and there at the end of the cot between the shapes of my two feet I beheld a dreadful sight.

Two lidless eyes like black diamonds fixed mine. A snake's gold-hooded head flared there, rising steadily from the floor. I dared not move, and hollering wouldn't help. *It is scareder of you than you are of it,* I remembered Mama saying and wished to high heaven she was in this cot in place of me. Poised as if to strike, the scaly critter continued to rise until the awful shadow of its hooded head fell across my feet. I had a mouthful of quilt by then, and every small sin I'd ever committed in my life passed before me.

I must have blinked despite myself. Gray light sparked upon the reptile's head, and I saw it was only the image of a snake, a cobra cleverly carved from some smooth blue stone. Rising before me was the face of a young girl, and on her head was this cobra crown. It was a narrow band of solid gold encircling her forehead, and the eyes in the terrible stone cobra's rearing head were diamonds indeed.

Her face rose from the shadows and now her neck, bedecked in a glittering collar. And now her bare shoulders, swarthy as a peach. She stood at the foot of my cot in a narrow white garb glimmering in woven gems.

Falling from her snaky headdress her black hair hung in long ringlets tightly coiled and set about with small precious beads that sparked red-and-blue fire. Her eyes found mine. Shadowed in paint as black as night they were almond-shaped and yellow. The brilliance of her eyes and the jewels lit up the attic. I'd never beheld such terrible beauty.

Drawing down my quilt with trembling hands I tried to speak, though my lips were dry and my tongue was turning.

"H-h-howdy do," I managed.

She might have been a painted statue before, but now her head moved forward in a little show of interest. Her long coiled tresses stirred, and the beads in them clicked.

In a voice like honey from the comb she spoke. "Why have you resisted me?" she said.

Her hands came up, cuffed in bracelets and bedizened with rings. She clasped them before her small but perfect bosom.

"Never have I appeared before a mortal. Now I do so out of desperation and some strange skill within yourself to call me forth."

"Who, me?" I said. "I—I—I don't believe I've had the pleasure."

She smiled then, or seemed to. "But you have," she said. "I am Hathor."

My mind whirled. H A T H O R. I wished to goodness I'd burned down that doggone Ouija board instead of the privy.

"Among my people," she said, silent as snow, "Hathor is the goddess of love."

My brain did somersaults. "Among the . . . Egyptian people?" I hazarded.

Her brightening eyes gave me the answer. "And that makes you a g-g-goddess?" I wondered.

There came the sound of light laughter then, temple bells. She shook her black tresses, and the cobra glanced from side to side. "No, no," she protested. "I am named for her. My whole name is Sat-Hathor, which means Daughter of the Goddess of Love. I am a princess." She looked down at her glittering garb.

"Imagine that," I replied, though it cleared up very little.

"And who are you?"

"B-Blossom," I bumbled.

"Blossom," she mused. "Like a flower?"

"More or less."

"Are you considered beautiful?" she inquired, her yellow eyes searching me.

"I am on the plain side, but I don't let it get me down." I paused, trying to sort out this strange happenstance. "Tell me one thing, Princess. Who might your papa happen to be?"

Her painted eyebrows rose to her crown. Though she was no taller than me when I'm standing, she drew herself up. "Sesostris the Second, Son of the Sun and Mighty above All Lesser Nations."

I froze. The name of Sesostris rang a bell for me, because I pay attention in Miss Fairweather's class, unlike some people I could mention.

When I could speak, my voice wobbled. "Then that puts you in or around the twelfth dynasty." She didn't deny it. "Princess, I've got some bad news for you. You've been dead right around three thousand eight-hundred years, more or less."

Her hand came up to still my words. "Not death," she corrected. "The Sleep of Death. Some things are eternal, but death is not one of them."

"I beg your pardon," I said. "Besides, you look in topnotch shape, all things considered."

She paused, puzzled. Then she put her head back and tinkled a hearty laugh. "It is not my earthly self you see. It is my ka."

"Ka?"

"I am the spiritual self of the Princess Sat-Hathor. My earthly self is . . . somewhere . . . elsewhere."

"Ah," says I, "then I'm looking at your soul."

"I will not bandy words with you," she said quite regal. "*Ka* will do."

"But you're more than a vision," I noted. "You seem solid enough."

For proof she thrust out a no-doubt sandaled foot and gave my chamberpot under the cot a convincing kick. It thunked roundly and clumped on the floorboards.

Another thought struck me. "As I understand it, you old—you folks spoke a foreign tongue which only scholars can decipher thanks to the Rosetta Stone. How come you and me can shoot the breeze?"

A puff of morning wind came through the missing windowpane, and she glanced aside, briefly confused.

"Oh, but you and I speak the same language. My people prepare ourselves for the future beyond our earthly lives, and you are a girl of the future. You and I hear each other clearly, for we speak from our hearts. They leave us our hearts, you know, when they prepare us for burial."

"Is that a fact," I remarked. "But see here, Princess. My particular Gift doesn't work that way. I've been known to pass back and forth through time. But I go to these times. They don't come to me. I don't get visitations from the dead—I mean to say, people presently resting."

"Oh, but I don't rest." Her hands came up to cup her cheeks. "How can I? For my tomb has been robbed of everything beautiful and necessary and my earthly self has been ripped from its sarcophagus. All that is me and mine has been carried away in the night by thieving hands."

"Grave robbers!" I said. "Them villains."

The bejeweled being at the foot of my cot quivered in rage and sorrow. "All the lovely things meant for my Afterlife are scattered by these jackals across lands unimaginable. Early and late they rob and remove us until they sift all the sands of the desert and leave us defiled!"

"Hardly a tomb has not suffered desecration unspeakable," I said in sympathy.

Dawn light began to find my attic, glowing upon Sat-Hathor's jewels: garnets and amethysts and gems I couldn't name. But she was still mourning for her earthly riches and self, pinched from her distant tomb.

I saw she was one tormented ka, but I wondered what to do. "Since you qualify as a ghost," I said, "you ought by rights to appear before Alexander Armsworth. He has a slight touch of the Second Sight and can see the . . . departed." In my mind I was still blaming that dad-ratted Ouija board for sending me this wrong number.

"A-lek-sander?" she said. "The name is Greek to me. Is he your husband?"

That gave me a turn. "Have a heart," I said. "We're only freshmen."

"How old would that make you?" She stroked her perfect chin with a long finger fitted with a false nail of purest gold.

"Fourteen."

Her eyebrows arched again. "I am fifteen, eternally. I was married at ten. My husband was twelve."

I blushed at the thought.

"Are you the last blossom blooming on the vine?"

"What? Oh, no. We don't marry off until somewhat later around here."

"Around here," she echoed sorrowfully, gazing about the brightening attic. I wondered if sunlight would scare her off, since she'd been in the shade, so to speak, for thirty-eight centuries. But the sun's rays flashed red on her lips, and she seemed to flower in the warmth on her face. Of course she comes from a hot country. "Around here," she moaned, "so far, so far. Rather a backwater too."

Then she heard a sound that I did not. Looking up at my slanting ceiling in sudden fear, she flinched and clapped her hands over her ears.

"What is it?" I half rose from my cot.

"The diggers draw nearer," she whimpered. "I hear their sharp spades ringing stone. They have found the steps that descend into darkness. Soon now they will find the broken seals on the door of my tomb. Soon they will stand within my robbed chambers and find me gone!"

"You can hear all that from here?"

"Oh, clearly," she explained. "My ka wanders between the broken door of my tomb and the gates of Yaru which is our paradise. And now, suddenly after centuries, I am here in this place with you. Therefore you must have some use to me."

I shrank somewhat, but she couldn't get those diggers off her mind.

"Soon they will find my sarcophagus and scrape the heavy lid away. And then, oh, woe, they will find nothing inside where my poor pilfered earthly self should be!"

"Your mummy," I murmured.

"*Earthly self* will do."

Her head swayed within her gold-tipped hands while authentic tears ran black down her face, striping her cheeks. It was pitiful.

"A princess is proud." She wept. "How shall the heathen diggers know that once Sat-Hathor lay in her rightful tomb surrounded by her full glory? They will stride about my sacred sepulchre as in an animal's rough cave. Never now will they remove me to some proud place like a palace where the multitudes may do me honor. I like honor. I am a princess."

My mind was whirling a mile a minute. *Diggers*, I thought. She must mean those Egyptologists like the well-known Sir Flinders Petrie. As I understand it, they aren't out to rob these tombs for personal gain. They're looking for high-class, well-equipped mummies to put in museums. Then the general public can do them honor. I pondered.

The sun flooded in the window, and Princess Sat-Hathor's white gown began to swim in many colors. Her edges blurred, and she seemed about to leave me. I felt a sudden pang.

"But, Princess," I said, "how can I find all your earthly goods and self scattered throughout lands unimaginable? Why me?"

"If not you, who?" She grew very solid again, wringing her hands and blazing in all the colors of a warm climate. "Time grows short. In only days my burial chamber will be discovered, uncovered. Before then, I must be found and all my goods, every scrap!"

"But what if I can't?" I began to sink beneath my quilt.

"We are well known for our curses," she warned. "Surely you've heard." I sank up to my eyes in the quilt. "On the other hand we can be generous to those who do our bidding."

She began to blur again, though not around the eyes. Even the cobra's diamond pinpoints grew sharper. Her glance traveled around the attic one more time.

"Are you a girl of the common people?" she asked.

"I am a little below them, to tell you the truth," I admitted.

"Then the usual rewards would not suit you. I take it you have no use for slaves or a nice river barge?"

I gaped.

She sighed a little. "Though this territory is as unknown to me as Mesopotamia, I will try to linger around your life to learn what you might like. If you help me, you will not find me ungrateful." Her fading face fell into shadow then and darkened fearfully. "But if you fail me, you'll rue the day you were ever born."

There came the distant sound of temple bells, or light, bitter laughter. Her eyes hung in the room a little longer than the rest of her. Then she was invisible. Whether she was gone or not is another matter. I sat up in my cot, chilled and stunned, while everything around me was less real than the Princess Sat-Hathor had been.

But a rude jolt soon brought me around. Glancing down I saw Mama's snaggle-toothed head popping up at the top of the ladder.

"Girl," she said, "what in blue blazes is this thing doin' in yore sack of sassafras?" In her claw she held up the dead butt of Alexander's cigar.

She flipped it across the attic floor and declared, "If I ever catch you lightin' up one of them things, you'll be blowin' smoke out of the back of yore head." With a wagging chin she disappeared into the floor. "And git off to school before I tan yore hide," she hollered from her underworld. "I don't want the law on me."

Too true, I thought, climbing weary from my cot. All the way to school I cursed lightly and hoped I wasn't. I had a mission to fulfill now which was worse than any Mama could dream up.

8

FORTUNATELY IT WAS A FRIDAY. A MONDAY would have been too much for many of us. After the night I'd put in, I was barely there. Maisie Markham wobbled into homeroom in worse shape still. Big though she is, she appeared drawn and hollow-eyed, as if somebody had taken a stomach pump to her. Letty was a bundle of nerves and sat twitching in her desk. Alexander was nearly late.

His collar was fresh, and he wore one of his sweaters in the argyle pattern. But when he made his faltering way down the aisle, he weaved from side to side. He was no longer the color of a gourd, but he was green around the gills.

I sat at my desk with hands clasped, waiting to see if his bleary eyes could focus. Just as he was about to flop into his seat, he managed to see me.

"Oh, gee whiz," he said sadly, and ran a hand through his blond mop. "Oh well." He sighed.

Looking from side to side shiftily, he stretched

his neck across my desk like a giraffe, and his pale lips puckered.

He was about to plant a required kiss on my forehead. But I sat up suddenly straight, practicing good posture, and he planted a quick wet one square on my mouth. His eyes had been tight shut, but now they flew open.

"And good morning to *you*, Alexander," I said quite perky. Already he'd wrenched himself back and collapsed into the seat ahead of me, where he seemed to be wiping his mouth with his sweater sleeve. A terrible crashing sound came from Letty's direction as she brought both her fists down on her desk top, jangling the inkwell. Then she used one of the worst polling-place words I've ever heard uttered in my life.

As the day ground on, Maisie was excused from biology, and I sat through English fighting heavy eyelids. I only stayed alert by concentrating on the back of Alexander's neck. There were a few singed hairs just where his blond mop curls down over his collar. Otherwise he seemed none the worse for his instructive experience. He was not a happy boy, however.

I was feeling no better, what with the curse of Princess Sat-Hathor hovering over my head. And her ka might be hanging around, too, for all I knew. By the time we got to history I wondered if a solution to this mess might rest with Miss Fairweather. After all, my problem was historical, and history is this learned woman's field.

In class that day she was describing to us the splendors of the great temple of Luxor when the door flew open. No teacher in the high school hates being interrupted more than her. Though a massive figure filled up the doorway, Miss Fairweather finished her thought. Only then did she pause and turn her stately head to the door. In tramped Old Man Leverette.

Even those who didn't know him goggled. A schoolroom is the last place you'd expect to see this elderly hayseed. He wore a tremendous pair of bib overalls and a farmerish straw hat. Miss Fairweather stared at the hat until he took it off.

"What is the meaning of this invasion, my man?" she inquired.

Old Man Leverette's eyes popped when he caught sight of her monocle. "Well, ma'am, I've suffered considerable loss of property at the hands of one of the br—boys in this here school." He turned the ragged brim of his hat in thorny hands.

Miss Fairweather considered that. "What manner of property?"

His ruddy face flushed deeper. Already Alexander was beginning to sink in the seat ahead of me. I could see everything right over his head. "Oh, gee whiz," I heard him faintly whisper.

"Some little son-of-a—little fellow was smokin' and burned down an . . . outbuilding, if you take my meaning."

Stiff as stone, Miss Fairweather nodded. "And

you are going from classroom to classroom, looking for the miscreant?"

"That is about the size of it," Old Man Leverette said in a low roar.

"An unorthodox plan," she noted. "I take it you are a taxpayer?"

"And how," he said.

"Then you may search this public schoolroom, and if he is here, you can have him."

You could hear a pin drop. By now Alexander had shrunk to the size of a dwarf.

Smelling of the barnyard and a recent fire Old Man Leverette started down the rows, scanning us. His gaze skipped over us girls, along with Collis Ledbetter, who's so small you never notice him. By now Alexander was practically sitting on the back of his neck.

Old Man Leverette took his time, picking the rows clean. Just before he came to ours, I reached down in my pocket and pulled up the butt of Alexander's cigar. Tying it with a broken rubber band I had handy, I leaned forward and dangled the incriminating butt over Alexander's low shoulder.

Already blind with fear he didn't notice it at first. I reached around and dangled it nearer his nose. He shot up and whirled around. "How?" he whispered in terror. "When?"

I smiled, snapping back the cigar and popping it into my pocket. Rage replaced the fear in Alexander's face. He was fixing to light into me, but thought better of it. Old Man Leverette was looming large in our aisle.

But he never slowed as he passed the paralyzed Alexander and peered beyond me to the next suspect of the male sex. Evidently, Alexander was looking near enough normal again to pass unrecognized. Old Man Leverette worked the room without luck and was heading out the door before Miss Fairweather spoke.

"I wish you justice, my man, though it is always in scant supply."

At that he turned back and said very civil, "Thank you kindly, ma'am. I regret any inconvenience to yourself." It sounded nothing like him, and he made a small bow with a sweep of his old straw hat, which wasn't like him either. Then he tramped off.

"The temple at Luxor," Miss Fairweather continued cool as a cucumber, "was greatly expanded in the time of Queen Nefertiti, and its construction was well in advance of modern-day methods. No, Maisie, you may not be excused."

She concluded with one of her threats regarding our Egypt projects. They were to begin nearly at once. We all quaked, for there's no playing for time with Miss Fairweather.

When the bell rang, Alexander hung back. If you have something people want, they're all over you, and he wanted that cigar butt back bad. I brushed past him, but he dogged my footsteps. Even when I approached Miss Fairweather, he hung back only a little. I sensed him there.

"Well, Blossom," she said in her brisk way, "I trust you have come up to tell me the topic of your project."

"You read my mind," I said, while she gave a small smile.

"I hope it is not to be pyramids, for I expect many projects on them from the less original students."

I waved the notion away. "Pyramids proved virtually worthless for storing royal mummies and their treasure. Even in ancient times many a mummy was removed from a pyramid and spirited away to some secret tomb in one necropolis or other."

Miss Fairweather's eyebrows rose. "I see you take your studies seriously, Blossom. I like that."

"I'm thinking of taking up Egyptology as a career," I said, suddenly deciding. "Now, you take Sir Flinders Petrie—"

"You are familiar with his work?" Miss Fairweather was mildly astonished.

"Even as we speak," I said, "he's digging for the remains and relics of the ancients to amaze us moderns."

"How true," she said. "I have recently read he is digging at Luhan in search of the tomb of a royal personage from the twelfth dynasty. What is your topic, Blossom?"

"Well, now," I said, "where do you stand on Ancient Curses, Miss Fairweather?"

She looked far down her nose at me. "Piffle," she said. "Nonsense passing as folklore."

"I'm glad to hear it," I said sincerely.

"I am waiting for your topic, Blossom."

"Well, now," I said, "there's always the subject of grave robbing through the ages."

Miss Fairweather swooped on that one. "Now, there is a worthy study to get your teeth into, and historically respectable. Just think of the priceless works of art purloined and passed from hand to worthless hand! Just think of the mummies themselves dragged from their rightful rest and put to some truly degrading uses!"

Just think, I thought.

"To do this topic justice," she warned, "you will have to do a very detailed project, Blossom."

I agreed. "Too detailed for one person." Sudden silence fell behind me as Alexander seemed to freeze on one foot. "I'll need to work with another student in a spirit of teamwork." I jerked my thumb in Alexander's direction. Miss Fairweather looked past me at him.

"Alexander Armsworth," she rang out, "are you willing to work with Blossom? It would seem your best and only chance for a good grade." Her eyes narrowed intelligently. "Besides, I believe you've just had a narrow escape in this classroom today. You need a heavier load of schoolwork to safeguard the property of honest taxpayers from your idle hands."

Turning to him myself, I slipped my hand into the pocket with the cigar in it, in case he needed further encouragement. His hair hung down over his trapped eyes, and he stubbed the floor with his boot toe.

"Oh, gee whiz," he whined, "I guess I'll have to."

So that's how me and Alexander formed a committee of two to work up our Egypt project on the outrage of Egyptian grave robbing.

When I got him to walk me home that afternoon, I gave him back his cigar as a pledge of faith. But was he grateful? Ha.

"Now I'll have to light up that thing again and smoke it all the way down," he grumbled. "The Iota Nu Betas have high standards."

"You should drop that bunch of oafs like a bad habit, Alexander," I advised. "They could all be implicated by name for burning down private property."

Alexander sighed. "Blossom, I don't want to blackmail them. I want to *join* them. Besides, I suppose it was me who set that fire, though I don't see how. I was careful to knock my ash right down the—"

"Not careful enough."

"And how do you know so much about it anyhow, Blossom? And how did you come by this cigar? I guess you were snooping on me again. With you around I am a hunted man."

I smiled mysteriously.

"If you'll give it some thought," I told him, "you might figure out how I can be in two places at once, maybe more. After all, you, too, have certain Powers out of the ordinary, if you'd admit it. You've seen ghosts—and don't bother to deny it."

He stumbled on smooth sidewalk. Any mention of this quirk of his throws him for a loop.

"I've told you before, Blossom, all that business is behind me. It was only a phase I was going through, and now I am back to normal and feeling first rate." He put more distance between us and stumped along down Pine Street, hurrying.

"Well, your social life and your Psychic life are your own, Alexander," I said mildly. "But me and you have a history project to pull off."

With shoulders squared Alexander maintained his pace. "You dig all that stuff out of your library books, Blossom, since you're such a big-time Egyptologist. I will come in at the last minute and help you put the finishing touches to it." Alexander spoke over his shoulder, and I had to skip along to keep up with him.

We were crossing his property at a fast clip. At the back of it stands the Armsworths' brick barn. This outbuilding is still known locally as the Ghost Barn because Alexander once saw a he-knows-what in it. The shadow of the barn fell across our path, slowing his steps.

"Not everything we need to know is in books," I said.

"Well, then, how are we supposed . . ."

His tongue went dead in his mouth. "Oh, no, Blossom. You won't catch me dabbling in . . . Matters Better Left Undabbled With. This is schoolwork we're talking about, and we must be strictly on the up and up. For one thing, it wouldn't be fair to the other freshmen who don't have any Special Powers, not that I do." Now the streetcar tracks were before us, and Alexander was throwing on his brakes. "This is as far as I go," he said, planting his boots.

"The secret membership of Iota Nu Beta," I said, "consists of Wendell Burdick, Monroe Puckett, Orville—"

"All right, all right. I'll walk you as far as your door, and that's my final offer."

"The back door," I bargained.

When we'd circled my house, I said with a sigh, "Well, Alexander, I see you won't be able to apply yourself to your schoolwork until you get this Iota Nu Beta business off your mind."

"It's an important issue." He sniffed.

"Now, let me think," I said. "As far as your initiation is concerned to date, you've got the toothbrush and kissing parts nailed down." Alexander reddened. "But you botched up the cigar smoking." He simmered. "And if they're going to pen you up in another privy . . ."

"They are," he admitted gloomily. "They said so."

"Well, if they give you your choice of privies," I said, "you could do worse than choose this one."

I gestured at the outhouse on the back of our property. Though me and Mama are without most luxuries, we have a landmark among privies. Being a two-holer, ours is double wide. It cast quite a substantial shadow across our weedy lot.

Alexander's eyes widened. He hadn't noticed it before, as on his side of the tracks they make other arrangements. I let him look. He could see for himself that such a sizable structure was less stuffy for smoking in. It wasn't exactly a parlor car on the Wabash Railroad, but it would take more time to smother in than your average outhouse. By then he ought to have his cigar smoked down if he kept puffing. This truth dawned on him.

"Of course, if you're to use it," I warned, "you'd better not burn it down. One open air outhouse in the community is enough."

Hope glinted in Alexander's face. Any fool could read his mind as he began to see that fraternity pin almost within reach. He turned from me thoughtfully, and I let him go. I had him on the hook, and now I must reel him in. With Miss Fairweather leaning on me from one side and the Princess on the other, I could not be expected to go it alone.

If I was to avoid a fatal curse, it looked to me like Alexander was going to have to be made ac-

quainted with the Princess Sat-Hathor—if not in
the flesh, in the ka.

From nowhere at all I heard the silvery sound of
temple bells lightly laughing on the evening air.
There were weird vibrations, and they were drawing nearer. I smiled uncertainly.

9

THROUGH THE LONG EVENING I SAT IN A POOL of lamplight and applied myself to my studies. Since Mama was out on her usual rounds, I passed the lonely hours by poring over my library books and making scholarly notes.

Near the chill hour of midnight I'd begun to grow drowsy when I heard stealthy footsteps out back. Turning down the wick on the lamp, I stole to the back window and peered out into the night.

It was the entire secret membership of Iota Nu Beta skulking away from our outhouse. Now they were hunkering down in the bald yard to keep an eye on the privy door. I had no doubt that a wisp of cigar smoke would shortly rise from it. Not for the first time I marveled at the strange ways of the male sex. Resting my elbows on the windowsill I settled to watch this dull drama unfold.

But it took no time at all. Before Alexander could have got his stogie going good, the night erupted

with his screams. *"Yeow!"* he screeched, sending
the night birds up from every tree in the vicinity.
The Iota Nu Betas, just now lighting up themselves, jerked to attention.

"Save me or I'm a goner," Alexander shrieked as
our privy door banged open and out he plunged.

An early frost had whitened the yard, and there
in silhouette I witnessed one of the strangest sights
of my experience. In this black-and-white scene
like a moving-picture show, Alexander seemed to
suffer a sudden bout of St. Vitus's dance. The cigar
leapt from his hand and fizzled out on the frosty
ground. Onward he danced, flinging and flailing
across the yard.

Draped around his jerking neck appeared to be
a narrow fur piece of the sort Mrs. Shambaugh
wears, but longer. Arms like windmills and head
bobbing, Alexander capered into the midst of the
Iota Nu Betas. They fell away from him, stumbling
and yipping like frightened puppies.

But hark! It wasn't a fur piece around Alexander's neck at all. It was, oh, no, Mama's missing
puff-adder snake, alive and well. I knew that thing
couldn't be far off. It writhed in a rhythm of its
own, trying to throw coils around Alexander's arm.
Its repulsive head was rearing back and puffing up.
Though the snake was somewhat rattled, it was not
scareder of Alexander than he was of it.

He did a quick back-step and a shimmy, hoping
to sling the puff adder over his head. Then he did a
number of deep bows to rid himself of the reptile.

Like all boys faced with danger the Iota Nu Betas scattered in every direction, pounding off around the house to save themselves.

The snake looped suddenly over Alexander's quaking head, fell like a collapsing tire on the white ground, and slithered off. Blindly, Alexander took a staggering step toward our back door.

I was there to open it as he tottered inside, gibbering with fear. His eyes looked like two burnt holes in a blanket. He took a few feeble steps across the floor before I slid a chair in under him.

The kettle was hot, so I poured him out a mug of sassafras tea to bring him around. His white lips nibbled at the rim of the mug before he could get down a swallow. As sassafras tea is better for you than it tastes, Alexander's eyes watered. Shortly he began to revive, for he started accusing me.

"D-d-dad-rat you, Blossom Culp. You knew. You lured me into that p-p-place, and you knew a boa constrictor was wrapped around the rafters just waiting to drop on me." His face went out of focus, and his voice broke in every direction. "Which it did."

"I didn't know any such thing, Alexander." It dawned on me the puff adder had no doubt been up there on my own visits to the privy. Maybe it was Alexander's cigar smoke that disturbed it. Still, if I'd ever thought to look up while in there . . .

Observing my troubled face Alexander was half convinced. His breath was still coming in gasps, and his hair was standing up in a halo about his head.

While I turned up the lamp and took a poker to the puny fire, he began to look suspiciously around the room. He'd never been inside my house before, and now he examined it: all Mama's herbs and the garlic onions hanging down in snaky bunches, the deck of greasy cards laid out on the table under my books, and the bushel baskets of assorted items Mama has tidied up from the community. There was also a brand-new matched set of lucky rabbit's-feet.

"Where's your mama now?" he asked, still suspicious.

"Working her night shift," I said, while Alexander began poking through her plunder.

"Now, what would she want with a thing like this?" He fished up a large roll of pasteboard tickets that all read: ADMISSION 10¢. Then he fished up a flimsy, glittering item. "And who'd wear a thing like that?"

It stopped me in my tracks, as I was reminded of the Princess's gleaming garb. But on closer inspection it was only a tacky brassiere with cheap sequins stuck on it, like a pony girl's in a circus. Discovering its shapely shape, Alexander dropped it and blushed.

"Your mama has the stickiest fingers in the state," he declared, and I couldn't deny it. At least he seemed to be recovering from his shock somewhat. Still, I didn't like his color. Taking down a small brown bottle I shook out a pill for him to swallow.

Alexander drew back. "Is that one of your mama's potions?"

"It's only a common aspirin. Mama doesn't dose herself with her own cures."

"I suppose I better take it. I still hear hissing in my head."

Bye and bye I got him settled down. The two of us sat not far apart in the almost cozy lamplight. Hoping to make this mellow moment last, I turned to our history project, as it was time he got serious about it.

"It's a confounded outrage, Alexander, what these grave robbers down the ages got up to. Did you know they used to grind up those mummies and sell them for medicine throughout Europe?"

He eyed the aspirin bottle with alarm.

"And another thing, it's well known that the best quality paper comes from linen rags. Just guess where they often got those rags from? Yessir, from the wrappings on the mummies. Many a book was made from the winding sheets of the dead!"

Alexander's eyes widened, but not at my knowledge. From the corner of my eye I saw something stir on the table, a flutter of paper. Against my will I turned to see Sir Flinders Petrie's *Ten Years' Digging in Egypt*. Its pages were turning. By themselves. And it wasn't the wind.

Speechless, we watched those pages flipping over as by an invisible hand. Of course I was not too shocked after the first moment. Such things are bound to happen in Alexander's vicinity, for he has a Gift and refuses to take responsibility for it. Anything is liable to happen with him around.

"I better be getting h-h-home," he breathed.

But I was on my feet, drawn to the book laid open at a large picture. Hoping the page had come to rest I bent nearer. It was an actual photograph of various small items dug out of a recently discovered tomb. They were called scarabs, and I recognized them at once.

Still, I read in a wavering voice Sir Flinders on the subject: " 'The Egyptians held the lowly dung beetle in high esteem. It was their symbol for eternity and figured prominently in their artwork. Precious stones were polished and carved in the configuration of this insect to insure safe passage into the Afterlife.' "

"We had a problem with beetles at our house," Alexander said faintly behind me. "But we put down poison and got rid of them."

Awestruck, I stood recalling a certain souvenir last seen in a certain shroud. Scarab was its name. I remembered the glowing color of it and thought of rubies.

"Mama has one of them scarabs," I told Alexander, speaking low for the drama of it. "She filched it from somewheres and was carrying it on her person the last time I looked."

Alexander's eyes skated around the room as if

Mama would soon be upon us, which she might. "It is probably a fake," he said.

"It was carved from a ruby as big around as a twenty-five-cent piece."

"Red glass, probably," Alexander muttered. "Like a taillight. Why do you want it, anyhow? We can use this picture from the book for our project if we need it. I'll hold up the book, and you can lecture the class about beetles or whatever. That'll be a fair shake."

"Listen, Alexander." I made so bold as to grab his arm. "I need that scarab bad, and I need to know how Mama come by it. Otherwise I'll be fatally cur—"

"Well, I must be off now," he said, easing away. He was still worried about those self-turning pages and wanted to put some distance between him and them. "My mother will skin me if she finds me missing at this time of night."

And without so much as a kiss-my-foot Alexander was already across the room and reaching for the doorknob. He jerked open the door, and something like a breeze gusted in. The shadows of all Mama's hanging herbs wobbled, and the lamp burned brighter by itself. Then I heard temple bells. They weren't lightly laughing now. They were jangling.

Alexander banged shut the door and stayed on this side. "I—I—I will try the front door," he stuttered. "It—it—it's nearer my house." But he stood like his boots were nailed to the floor.

"What is it, Alexander?" I wasn't too anxious to go nearer the door myself.

"N-n-nothing at all." His hand was frozen on the doorknob. "That cigar has made me light headed."

"Then you better step outside and get a breath of fresh air."

Alexander whimpered.

But it didn't matter. The door was opening now, automatically, and Alexander was stumbling backward over the bushel baskets. The door fell back, and there, outlined by the night, stood the Princess Sat-Hathor in all her glory.

"Oh, glory." Alexander sobbed. His hands were plucking at his sweater front, and he was muttering to himself. "I will be a good boy for the rest of my life if only—"

"A-lek-sander," she said foreignly. Her bejeweled hand rose, and she pointed a golden fingertip square at him. She was nearer us somehow, and the door closed obediently behind her. Alexander was peeking out between his fingers now and lamenting his fate. The glittering eyes on her cobra crown didn't lift his spirits much either.

"Why do you shrink from me, A-lek-sander? Have you never looked upon one tormented and lost in Time?"

"N-n-never," Alexander swore, his eyes bugging at her brilliance.

"Tell the truth," I said from the side of my mouth. "She's wise to you."

"Oh, gee whiz." He sobbed.

"Where am I, A-lek-sander?" she asked, raising black brows.

"R-r-right there," he admitted miserably.

"Wrong," I muttered. "That's her ka you're looking at. She means her mum—earthly self."

"I don't know," he moaned. "I'm innocent."

Terrifyingly, her burning yellow eyes shifted to me. "Have you told him nothing, Flower?"

I cleared my throat. "Well, I was working up to it. You know yourself these things take time with a boy."

She nodded briefly and returned her fiery stare to him. "For centuries, A-lek-sander, I lay richly arrayed in the Sleep of Death, confident of eternity. But rudely I was robbed and cruelly I was torn from my tomb. Wickedly I was borne away over stormy seas to be made a mockery of by the common people."

She vibrated with outrage.

"And now, A-lek-sander, I lie coffinless where only the pitiless wind finds me. I feel this wind, but I cannot find me. Soon I will be more shamed still when the diggers in my homeland discover my violated tomb."

Alexander's eyes were like saucers, and his ears were out to here. It was just as I've always said, his Powers are such that the departed communicate with him first-rate. He understood every word, too, and maybe more, though he fought against it.

The lamp blazed brighter on the many gem colors of her face and garb. "Find me and see me home. It is my command to you both! The diggers are deafening, and I can hear them even from this dreadful distance. Time grows short, but not so short as the patience of a princess!"

She dimmed then, but she didn't vanish. We watched the darkness etch itself in the mummiform shape of an Egyptian coffin. It formed around her form, this coffin she'd been ripped from way off there in Egypt.

We saw the coffin lid as it should be, enclosing her. In brilliant color picked out in gleaming gold was the image of a sacred, yellow-eyed cat, and the falcon, too, with the mismatching eyes, who is god of the Afterlife. In scrolling shapes we saw a winged serpent whose coils wound away into infinity. Beneath at her feet, carved hugely, was a gilded scarab.

The lamp on the table dimmed at her bidding, and she was almost at one with the darkness. But she was still there like a reminder.

Though his boots were lead weights, Alexander whirled around and tried to make tracks. Kicking Mama's bushel baskets sky high, he plowed across the room to the front door.

He threw it open and screamed like a banshee. Mama was just coming home, and he'd very nearly run her down. She staggered on the threshold. A mostly empty croaker sack was on her back, and she'd tied a filthy flour bag over her head for a kerchief. She carried a broken-off branch for a walking stick.

As Alexander dodged past her, she fetched him a terrific thwack with her branch across the seat of his knickers.

"Git outta here, you little owl-hoot." Grunting, she banged the door shut with a backward kick.

I looked from her to the Princess Sat-Hathor. When she saw Mama, she glowed brighter again, especially around the eyes, staring with quite human curiosity. As I've often said, Mama's a sight to raise the dead.

"We have company," I remarked to her.

"Yes, and if I catch that squirt in here again, I'll wear you both out with this." She shook her branch aloft.

"I didn't mean Alexander," I said with patience. "Mama, I'd like to make you acquainted with Princess Sat-Hathor of the twelfth dynasty, daughter of Sesostris the Second."

Mama's chin met her nose as she squinted around the room. Though the Princess's jeweled white gown lit up the place, Mama's gaze swept right past her. Then she shambled over and scooped my books off the table to ease her sack down.

"Girl, you're talkin' out of yore head agin. I bin meanin' to speak to you about that."

The room filled with tinkling, timeless laughter before the Princess faded.

So much for Mama's proud supernatural powers.

10

TIME IN ITS TROUBLESOME WAY BEGAN TO hang heavy on my hands. In my books I'd learned about the tortures the old Egyptians performed on any victims who displeased them. I won't describe these tortures here, as they don't make pleasant reading.

For the first time in my life I began sleeping with a night-light, and I was scared of my own shadow. While beautiful, the Princess's ka was growing desperate and dangerous. Since she and her belongings were scattered throughout lands unimaginable, I despaired of giving her a helping hand. The only likely clue was that ruby scarab. But when I checked Mama's shroud the next chance I got, the mysterious carved gem was gone.

At least the Princess's curse now hung over Alexander too. But this was scant consolation if we were both to be cursed from here to eternity. And doubtless Alexander had spent a busy weekend denying to himself he'd witnessed the Princess in all her glory. Though his Powers are strong, his will is not.

Sure enough, on Monday morning Alexander looked right past me in homeroom and English. But in history class me and him figured prominently.

Word had circulated that us two were doing our project in tandem. Not quite speechless with rage, Letty announced to all and sundry that she was no longer talking to Alexander. "Faithless worm" was one of her terms for him.

Everybody in Miss Fairweather's class wanted to copy me and Alexander by forming committees to lighten their loads. She was inclined to agree in the interest of producing better results. Big Belcher Cunningham's bunch of boys began working together on a strictly scientific demonstration of mummification, using Collis Ledbetter as the corpse of a small pharaoh. Having no choice, Collis joined this committee.

Miss Fairweather had to step in to organize the duller scholars into building a replica of the Great Pyramid at Cheops, and she was hanging over them till they got it right.

Letty organized all the S.T. & B.F.S. girls to work up a living tableau with authentic details on the death of Queen Cleopatra. It was to feature herself in the starring role and the other girls as handmaidens and slaves.

Letty had also changed the theme of the freshman Homecoming float from "Put the Bulldogs in the Doghouse" to the more historic "A-*Nile*-ate the Bulldogs." Her plan was to shift her class project onto a float for the parade. It would therefore do double duty, and she could play the starring role twice, once while barging down all the streets in town before the general public.

All her Sisterhood was busy creating a chickenwire-and-crêpe-paper barge, raiding their mothers for costume jewelry and feathers, experimenting with eye makeup, and stuffing a fake asp.

Though Miss Fairweather gave this committee plenty of stern warnings about making their project completely authentic, Letty was clearly warming up to our new teacher. Put Letty in the starring role of any situation, and she's cheery as a sunbeam.

While it took him a day or so, Alexander got around to speaking to me. Sidling up in the midst of history class he said, "Say, Blossom, I'm worried. Everybody else is putting together crackerjack projects. Look how Belcher's boys have got all those Red Cross bandages to tie up Collis with. And Letty's Cleopatra is going to be better than the moving pictures. Would you look at those costumes and that throne? Even the dunces are coming up with a pyramid to scale. I don't see how you and I are going to make much of a showing."

I sighed. "Alexander, you definitely take the cake. Here we two are under a heavy curse from a princess who plays for keeps, and all you can think about is showing off in front of the class."

Smoothing down his sweater he said, "I was in hopes the Princess might have taken a shine to me." Then he shot me a look that dripped with guilt. Without meaning to he'd confessed that he'd actually seen her. Though progress is slow with Alexander, here was one small step.

Still, I simmered. "Alexander, the Princess has but one thing on her mind, and that is—"

He put up a silencing hand. "As soon as I get a certain important matter taken care of, I'll be able to give our . . . situation some thought."

"If you're talking about being initiated into that two-bit fraternity . . ."

"I am," he said smugly, "and the big ceremony's tonight." He dripped with sudden guilt again for having given away this dark secret. "The Iota Nu Betas say they're tired of initiating me, so they're going to finish the job." He glanced furtively around.

"As for our little problem," he said with more confidence, "I suppose we'll have to work that out together. Not that this curse business worries me, because it is all piffling folklore."

Watch your mouth, I thought to myself.

"But if I can manage to locate the Princess's mummy somehow, you'll have to dream up a way of getting it back to her . . . tomb, or wherever. That'll be a fair shake."

Out of simple desperation I grew interested.

"Say, Alexander, have you got some special trance up your sleeve for finding—"

"Clam up about all that, Blossom." He took a backward step. "I am going to solve this mystery strictly on the up-and-up, using my powers of deduction."

I clutched my forehead. "Alexander, if you depend only on your reason, it could take years. We don't have that kind of time. There's nothing shorter than the patience of a princess, as you heard for yourself."

He set his jaw in a stubborn way. "Now, listen, Blossom, don't nag me. And don't even think about horning in on my initiation ceremony tonight. It is men only. Let this be a warning. If you meddle before I get this all worked out in my mind, I'll drop you like a bad habit."

Since Alexander was foolish enough to do just that, I decided to be patient, though it is not natural to me. On the night of his initiation ceremony you might have expected me to track him like an Indian scout despite his threat. But I decided against it. Instead, I carried three lamps up to my attic to brighten all its corners and hung an old sheet over my window, for all the good it would do. Then I settled into my cot to read *A Tale of Two Cities*, keeping strictly off anything Egyptian. I wouldn't have slept anyhow.

Long after Mama rambled in and flopped before the stove below, I was still deep in the French

Revolution. I heard nothing from the darkness outside before a pebble struck my windowpane. Jumping half out of my skin I stuck up my nose for a whiff of cedar and incense, but smelled nothing.

"Pssst, Blossom!" an all-too-human voice whispered loud from the yard. Drawing back the sheet at my window I saw below the faint blur of Alexander's blond mop. I stuck my head out.

"There you are. I was running out of pebbles." He seemed to shuffle his feet uncertainly. "I think you better come on down. There's . . . something I guess you better see."

As I don't get an invitation from Alexander every night, I slipped back for my old coat, blew out the lamps, and returned to the window.

"Get ready to catch me. I can't creep down the ladder in here without raising Mama."

That wasn't necessarily so, but I liked the idea of dropping on Alexander. While he braced his boots beneath my window, I swung out, dangled from the drainpipe, and turned loose. It was only a six-foot drop, but I didn't land as planned in his arms. During my fall I seemed to kick him in the head, and we both ended in a heap on hard ground.

We were shortly untangled and scuttling away. On the far side of the grove Alexander fetched up and with a trembling hand opened his coat. There on his chest, winking in moonlight, was his brand-new fraternity pin with the seed pearl. Though his chest puffed automatically to make it gleam, his thoughts were elsewhere. He reached down his sweater front and drew up a tightly rolled scroll.

"What do you make of this?" He unrolled it, and moonlight washed over it. "The Iota Nu Betas say this is a copy of their darkest fraternal secrets, but I wonder. They can't read it themselves. I think it was just something they grabbed up at the last minute."

My eyes widened. I couldn't read it, either, not without the Rosetta Stone. The ink was blurred, but it was ancient Egyptian writing of the hieroglyphic type. Though gibberish, it was artistic. The brittle paper was papyrus. I had no doubt it had been written by some ancient scribe in centuries gone by.

"Where, Alexander?" I huddled near him.

He wavered, but then said, "Come on, I'll show you. It's a weird place, but I'll protect you. Walk on ahead, and I'll hang back to cover our rear."

We tramped a moonlit mile or two out past the edge of town, over the Snake Creek trestle bridge and past Old Man Leverette's abandoned farm. My nose and toes were blocks of ice before we turned off a secondary road and rounded a stand of trees deep in the countryside.

There, lurid by moonglow, I saw a half-collapsed tent with its flaps flapping. A raggedy circus pennant or two still rippled in the breeze. Swinging like a black vine was a string of electric bulbs once bright but now empty sockets. Cast about in the tall weeds were once colorful sideshow posters, and a passing cow had made a mess of one.

"What on earth," I said of this unearthly scene.

"It was that tent show that folded last summer," Alexander said. "The Iota Nu Betas picked the spot for my initiation, as it's strictly private." Distracting himself he added, "Here they showed me their secret handshake and made me tell everything I knew about girls."

That couldn't have taken more than a minute, I mused. But I clutched Alexander's arm as something else dawned on me. "This spot may be strictly private, but Mama has found her way to it. Here's where she pinched those popcorn boxes and that glitter walking-stick and that sorry Kewpie doll. Where else?"

Alexander nodded in the night. "And that roll of ten-cent tickets," he said, "and that gaudy costume thing. I guess here's where she got the boa constrictor, too, that she caged up in your outhouse." He shuddered, perhaps with the cold.

"No, Alexander, that was only a common puff-adder snake that Mama dragged out of its hole," I explained. "And it was scareder of you than you were of it," I added.

Wind whined through the shaky tent. The trees beyond seemed full of night birds listening.

"And the beetle jewel," I said, barely aloud. "The blood-red scarab. It came from here, along with that scroll of yours."

"I'm afraid so, Blossom," Alexander said. "When the Iota Nu Betas finished up initiating me, they left me here as part of the ritual, to find my own way home. So I had a look around and . . . yes, Blossom, your mama found the scarab here."

"But why should a thing so valuable be in among such trash?"

Now I felt Alexander's hand close around my elbow, and he was leading me into the sagging tent. As in a dream there was no going back.

Inside were piles of canvas and mildewed pony bridles. Battered trunks yawned open, thoroughly rifled. "It is picked pretty clean," I murmured in homage to Mama.

"Not quite." Alexander's hand gripped me tighter. The Iota Nu Betas had left him a candle from their ceremony. With the book of matches I always carry in my shoe top we soon had it going. Its flame lit up the desolation dreadfully. I thought of how me and Alexander must look from outside with our huddled silhouettes showing through the worn canvas.

"Over there." He pointed to a mouse-nibbled bale of hay. Careful with the candle we drew nearer. A small leaflet torn halfway through lay in the rubble. As far as I could make out it read:

GAZE
Upon the mystery of the ages—
an authentic mummy of a beautiful
young woman dead a thousand years

before Solomon and Sheba!
SEE
for yourself a daughter of the
pharaohs well preserved by a now
lost process and accompanied by
a small but tasteful selection of
her worldly goods
    Inspiring! Educational! Entertaining!
      One Thin Dime Extra

"Oh, no," I said, too near at last.

"She's here," Alexander said, "left behind under that old hay bale. It was true that she'd been borne away over stormy seas to be made a mockery of by the common people."

My eyes stung with tears, though I can usually keep them back. "It isn't right, Alexander. She was no circus freak. She was a princess. She liked honor."

"I know. It's a rotten shame," he said, older than he is. "Would you like to . . . view her, Blossom?" His voice was kindly.

Beyond the hay bale was only a bundle of old rags. But we'd reached our goal. Bending on either side of the bundle we planted the candle at the head, her head.

"Maybe it isn't her," I whispered. "They often faked mummies. When they couldn't come by a real one, they'd make a kind of doll out of old leather and . . ."

Alexander was reaching down to the rags bandaged in an intricate pattern around a human form. The wrappings were loose, for hands before his and even Mama's had disturbed her. She'd been on the move no doubt for many weary years. And she'd been ripped asunder more than once.

But never by such gentle hands as Alexander's. Some of the linen frayed away at his touch, but he unwrapped her head with dignity. The candle bobbed and weaved, and the tent rumbled with wind. How long it took him I don't recall: an eternity it seemed.

At last in yellow candlelight we gazed down on the earthly self of the Princess Sat-Hathor, alone in this alien place. Her face was the color of a tobacco leaf, and her once cherry lips were a jagged line. Though her brow was noble still, it was grooved where the cobra crown had once bound her forehead. Her neck was now no bigger around than the circle of my finger and thumb. Her hair was there, black and glossy yet, with the little blue and red beads still plaited in place.

"Is she beautiful or awful?" Alexander wondered.

"Yes," I said.

It was the Princess Sat-Hathor, real in a world full of fakery. I suppose the years, the centuries, had been kind to her, considering. But she was shrunken now, a dry shell, an autumn leaf in this November night. I'd have known her, though. She was a princess still, and me and Alexander were on our knees before her.

Only her nose was not quite as it should have

been, for it had a bump on it. But, ah, I thought, that often happened when they drew out the brains through the nose in their mummification ritual. Remembering this interesting fact from my reading, I kept it to myself out of respect.

Though her tobacco-leaf face was drawn in a million dry wrinkles, her shut eyelids were full as if in pleasant sleep. But, ah, I thought, they often replaced the eyeballs beneath with small onions, which were precious to the Egyptians. Education is a wonderful thing, especially when it can keep you from being scared witless.

I reached out and touched her shoulder, brittle as papyrus and naked beneath the old linen. I thought of her bare within her bandages and had a vision of all her finery scattered across the years and empires. Without them, and without her in-nards, she wouldn't weigh much now, I mused.

"I don't suppose," Alexander said, "she'd be satisfied with a decent burial right here. We could put up a little stone and copy a hieroglyphic or two on it. We could make it nice."

I shook my head. "She wouldn't understand that. She's foreign."

"I don't suppose," he said, "you could sort of wish her back to Egypt or send her off with one of your spells?"

"Oh, Alexander, I don't know how. Anyway, you've kept your part of the bargain. You've found her. But was it purely by chance? Surely not."

Alexander thought. He was closer now than he'd

ever been to owning up to his Powers, him who works so hard to be as ordinary as everybody else. "I don't know. I guess it was just my fate that brought me here. Looks like I can no more explain it than I can escape it."

He cast a glance across the mummy at me. "And, Blossom, I won't drop you like a bad habit now. I'll do whatever I can to help you with the Princess. We're in this together, and I don't mind too much."

The candle burned low, but brighter in my heart. The wind whipped the tent above us, but I was warm as toast. I'd have stretched that moment to eternity, but then I had to say, "We can't leave her here, Alexander. One way or another she has a long journey before her, and at least we'd better get her out of the weather."

We stood up and planted our feet to heave her up, but up she came nearly floating, trailing a ragged bandage or two.

"Why, she hardly weighs a thing," he exclaimed.

"Well, she wouldn't," I lectured. "When she was mummified, they cut out her stomach, liver, lungs, and guts. Then they went to work and pickled them separately and put them into four fine alabaster jugs called 'Canopic jars.' They put her heart back in her, but it's probably no bigger than a dried fig now."

Alexander swallowed and glanced away from our burden. She hung between us, feather-light, and her young black hair with the beads clicking in it fell down from her aged brow. We bore her home between us over the trestle bridge and along the back roads to Bluff City, treating her with care, for her earthly self was more fragile than her ka. Shorter, too, as she was shrunk up some.

Alexander left me at my door, and I carried the princess into the dark house. If Mama heard, she made no sound or sign. Cautiously I eased my light load up the steep ladder. Then there was no room in the attic to stash her except under my cot. I scooted her dry husk in there with no more sound than a mouse moving.

"Well, Princess," I whispered in case her ka was near, "this isn't much, but it's the best I can do for the time being. Make yourself at home and try to be patient."

Her mummy, being brainless, said nothing.

Too tired even to skin off my clothes, I dropped on the cot into a deep sleep, just as if a dead body and I weren't stacked up like cordwood. I didn't dream, unless I dreamed that distant tinkle of temple bells.

11

WHILE ME AND ALEXANDER STILL LIVED BE-
neath a ka's curse and the diggers drew nearer a
pilfered tomb over in Egypt, a storm cloud began
to form over Bluff City High School.

On the very day we were to present our history
projects, the school hallways were filled up with an
angry posse of what looked like mothers. Enormous corseted forms filled the halls to overflowing,
and tremendous feathered hat brims overlapped.
Fur pieces hung down in profusion and appeared
to quiver with rage. These big women all but flat-
tened us scholars against the walls.

The ringleader of their warlike group was Mrs.
Shambaugh. Her hat was the biggest, loaded with
both ostrich plumes and wax fruit. Like Letty she is
always overtrimmed. She was tapping her foot outside the principal's office. His name is Mr. Moody,
which is lettered on the frosted glass.

All of us, young and old, surged forward to see if

his door would open, as none of us had ever set eyes on him before. Evidently there's no back way out of his office, for his knob finally turned, and the door opened a wedge. There stood the principal. Come to find out he's quite short. He looked a little like Collis Ledbetter grown, but not up.

Mrs. Shambaugh's gigantic shadow fell upon him. "Mr. Moody," she boomed down, "you see before you a deputation of prominent Bluff City ladies. We are the Daughters of the American Revolution, the Order of the Eastern Star, and other concerned citizens of the gentle sex drawn from old-settler families!"

Playing for time, perhaps, Mr. Moody withdrew a handkerchief from his breast pocket, removed his spectacles, and gave them a polish. Then he hooked them over his little ears and peered up. Huge hats were nodding in agreement with Mrs. Shambaugh all the way back to the main entrance.

"My stars," Mr. Moody said, gazing at their prows.

From her reticule Mrs. Shambaugh drew out a long sheet of paper like a proclamation and unfolded it before him.

"Here is our petition signed by the wives of prominent men and the mothers of endangered children!" She shook the petition. "A few of us are on the school board too," she added for good measure.

"What seems to be—"

"I'm coming to that," Mrs. Shambaugh trum-

peted. "Under your dubious direction this school is harboring a viper to its bosom." Her own swelled. "A certain Miss Fairweather, whom you have plucked from obscurity to twist the minds of innocent children with the snake oil of her suffragette scheming! If you are not in cahoots with this unnatural woman yourself, we will all be glad to hear why you have let this radical onto your faculty!"

"Land sakes," Mr. Moody murmured, "I thought Miss Fairweather was doing ancient Egypt with the freshmen."

"Ancient Egypt my Aunt Fanny," Mrs. Shambaugh blared. "These suffragette types will tell you anything to worm their way into schoolrooms and teach our kiddies filth! I trust you do not champion votes for women, Mr. Moody?"

"Good grief." He gulped. "No."

"I should think not. Yet we of the community are paying you one thousand dollars per annum to run a school of subversive suffragism," she bellowed moistly. "You will be out on your ear when *that* hits the headlines!"

Mr. Moody took on the look of a man whose pocket is just about to be picked in public. But I'd heard enough. Beneath the dangling fur pieces I darted away down the hall. By now we should all have been milling in homeroom, but Mrs. Shambaugh's voice had stilled even the electric-bell system. I galloped toward the history room to warn Miss Fairweather, for there was tar and feathers in Mrs. Shambaugh's eye.

When I skidded into the classroom, I found Miss Fairweather slumped at her desk. Even her starchy shirtwaist had begun to droop, and her pale hand rested on her throat. She looked tired to death, defeated nearly.

"Oh, Blossom," she said, hardly looking up. It's not a pretty sight to see such a proud woman brought down in this unfair way. She already knew they were out to get her, because you can hear Mrs. Shambaugh at any distance.

"And the principal will fold like a house of cards," she said, mostly to herself.

"It's a confounded outrage." I made a fist and shook it. "You don't teach us votes for women."

Her head came up a little. "I would have gotten around to it," she said. "That cause is history, too, or will be."

I stood before Miss Fairweather's desk helpless, which is not a thing I like to be. Then, when her hand drifted down from her neck, my eyes all but fell out of my face.

There on the collar of her white shirtwaist came a flash of ruby-red fire. I bent nearer. At her throat, set in a new little oval of gold jeweler's wire, was the Egyptian scarab. I'd last seen it hidden in Mama's shroud. Now, made up into a brooch, it hung on, of all people, Miss Fairweather.

Wordless, I pointed a finger as crooked as Mama's square at it. Miss Fairweather just touched the scarab again in an uncertain gesture.

"B-but that's an authentic Egyptian scarab," says I, "probably twelfth dynasty."

Her eyes skittered. "It is certainly very like one," she admitted. "By rights I ought not to be wearing it, but . . . it is so pretty." Her hand crept up to her severe hair in a strangely girlish move.

"Where in blazes did you get it?" I blurted.

She hesitated. "It seems to have come from an unknown gentleman admirer. I naturally intend to return it when I ascertain who . . . he is." She cleared her throat with a small sound. I was more stumped than ever.

But the shock of seeing that scarab again seemed to sharpen my vision. I looked around the classroom, where all our projects awaited presentation.

Belcher's pile of bandages for wrapping Collis were there in a heap. Somehow his bunch had even come up with a couple of urn-shaped table lamps to serve as Canopic jars for a mummy's innards. The dunces' sugar-cube Pyramid of Cheops was topping out in a corner. Littering the rest of the room were the many props for Letty's Cleopatra production.

Her throne was there, and strewn over half the desks were the fancy costumes for herself and her handmaidens. A narrow ray of morning light fell through the crack in the window blind and glinted goldenly upon a certain object among Letty's litter. My eyes widened when I saw what it was.

Then I was inspired, and a solution to Miss

Fairweather's problem appeared before me like a bolt from the blue.

"Blossom?" she said, seeing the state I was in.

I pulled myself together. "Miss Fairweather, we had better nip Mrs. Shambaugh in the bud and have us a showdown." I was already starting to the door, busy with my plans. "Let the principal and that entire gang of Mrs. Shambaugh's into our classroom. Invite them all in to see us demonstrate our Egypt projects. After all, they're taxpayers too."

Miss Fairweather stroked her scarab. "I suppose a little learning would do them no harm," she mused.

"And better yet," I replied, "I think what they learn will shut them up for eternity!"

"Mercy, Blossom, how you talk." But I was breezing right past her now. "I suppose I have little to lose from a showdown," she added.

"I'll have to be absent from school until time for our class," I said at the door. "Kindly cover for me till then. And Alexander too." Then off I darted with wings on my heels.

Luck was with me, for I ran smack into him. Soon we were both escaping, hand in hand, down the hallways bulging with mothers. Then we were outside and heading for home and a certain something that was waiting under my cot. For once, Alexander didn't waste time with questions or hang back in his usual way.

It was far from a typical day in history class that morning. Every prominent woman in Bluff City, us regular students, and all the paraphernalia for the projects threatened the floor with collapse. Mr. Moody took up a small space by the door, hoping for escape.

But don't think Miss Fairweather wasn't equal to the occasion. She'd removed the scarab brooch and secreted it somewheres. Now she stood severe while the room grew orderly. As she fitted her monocle over her eye, all the muttering mothers, even Mrs. Shambaugh, fell silent.

"We are honored," she said in a voice of ice, "to welcome visitors from this little community into our Halls of Learning." The prominent mothers shrank slightly. "We are sorry indeed that our visitors must stand, but our schoolroom furniture would hardly accommodate most of you." The mothers shrank more as Miss Fairweather's gaze fell upon Mrs. Shambaugh.

"In this class we are studying ancient Egypt, which has much to tell us about Civilization." With a snap of her fingers she sent the committee of slower scholars into action. They tramped over to their Pyramid of Cheops and beamed dimly down at their creation.

It didn't take Miss Fairweather long to spot several of these dunces' mothers. She singled them out and drew them away from Mrs. Shambaugh so they could be educated on pyramid construction. Though she was patient and precise with them, the terror grew in the mothers' eyes as if they feared a quiz coming.

When they'd learned as much as they could manage, Miss Fairweather turned to Belcher's project. His bunch was ready. They'd cleared off her desk top to stretch Collis out on the blotter. He was down to his B.V.D.'s, and they were wrapping him with Red Cross bandages in the intricate pattern favored by ancient priests. On various bandages they'd lettered in black ink *Pharaoh Collis I*, using the English language, as nobody knew how to spell his name in pictogram. Handy at Collis's little head and feet were the urns.

Belcher's boys naturally did not draw off Collis's brains or cut into him for his insides to put in these urns. But they had a sponge, a dish of sausages, about a pound of raw calf's liver, and an old sheep's bladder to stand for his interior parts. They also had a jar of Vaseline, representing the sacred ointment used to keep a mummy's skin supple for centuries. This they worked over his exposed areas. It was messy work, but educational. They'd even drawn a large sun on the blackboard to represent the seventy days of open-air drying every mummy needed.

Belcher Cunningham's mama was there. She drew nearer to witness this demonstration, also leaving Mrs. Shambaugh behind. Another mother joined Mrs. Cunningham at the desk. Peering down at the small pharaoh she exclaimed, "Why,

Collis, honey, what an honor!" So this must have been Mrs. Ledbetter.

When it came time for Letty's entrance, Mrs. Shambaugh was all but friendless. Having donned their costumes in the girls' restroom the S.T. & B.F.S. girls now trooped in and climbed onto their barge. Maisie, as largest handmaiden, wore an old costume of hers like gauzy bloomers and carried a big ostrich-feather fan to keep the flies off Cleopatra.

All the other girls, plastered with makeup, grouped around the fine throne. Adjusting her asp, Letty settled. The crown on her head drew every eye, and I'll have to admit that in her queenly raiment she never looked better. She shot her mother a warning look. Mrs. Shambaugh's fingers crept up to cover her own lips in a rare gesture.

Though Letty took her sweet time dying from the asp, Miss Fairweather moved us at last to the final project. "It is on the tragic topic of royal-grave robbing," she announced. "Blossom and Alexander, come forth!"

We were strictly on our own, as our mothers were not present. Mine for obvious reasons. His because Mrs. Armsworth has been kept out of every club in town by Mrs. Shambaugh for reasons of her own. Alexander looked troubled. All he knew was that we had the Princess's earthly self up our sleeve.

When Miss Fairweather turned the floor over to me, I took charge. Several of the mothers gave me

astonished once-overs. "Saints above," Mrs. Shambaugh muttered, "not Blossom."

"It's a rotten shame," I began, "how grave robbers down the ages have rifled the sacred tombs of
old Egypt for personal gain and a fast profit. The
mummies themselves have been dragged halfway
around the world, passing from hand to hand.

"Give me a hand," I whispered, nudging Alexander into action. We'd slid the Princess's mummy in
under Miss Fairweather's desk. Now it was time for
the unveiling.

"Roll off," I said to Collis on the blotter, "I've got
a real one."

Quick to obey, Collis rolled in his wrappings to
the edge of the desk. His mother, swooping forward, scooped him out of the air.

Then suddenly before the amazed throng, me
and Alexander replaced him with the mummy of
Princess Sat-Hathor in all her authenticity. A gasp
went up as the mothers surged forward. All the
Sisterhood girls swarmed off their barge for a view
and then fell back. Maisie's hand clapped over her
mouth.

"Gaze!" I commanded, "upon the actual
mummy of a beautiful young woman dead a thousand years before Solomon and Sheba!"

Everybody did. Even Mr. Moody left the door to
edge nearer, peering around the mothers. The
Princess lay before them, her empty self rocking
slightly like a giant cocoon, her bandages old and

weathered as her face, the scroll stuck back in with her where Alexander had replaced it.

"See for yourselves a daughter of the pharaohs, well preserved by the process you've just observed." I nodded civilly to Belcher, who gaped back.

"Great guns," his mother cried, "that thing ought to be in its grave!"

"How true," I said, "and her rightful belongings with her." I had this bunch in the palm of my hand as I looked about the room. "But where are the few remnants of her riches now?" I glared at my audience, for this was no idle question.

"Where are the precious possessions meant for this mummy's trip to eternity? By any chance at all were a few of them scattered around Bluff City when this sorry mummy was dumped by a tent show?"

You could have heard a pin drop as I turned to face Letty's barge. As if by chance my glance fell upon the fancy antique chair she'd brought from the Shambaugh residence for her throne.

Crooking a dramatic finger at it I said, "But hark! There stands an Egyptian chair, no doubt from the twelfth dynasty." And so it was without any doubt. Its paint was flaking artistically, and across its back was a fine carved design of winged serpents and sacred falcons.

A strangled sound came from the rear of the gazing group, possibly from Mrs. Shambaugh, the well-known antique collector.

"And hark!" I cried, pointing to the floor. "Is this alabaster urn which has been wired as an electric table lamp not in fact a real Canopic jar used to store the insides of an actual mummy? The tasteful hieroglyphics on its side tell its tale!"

Quick on his feet, Alexander slipped around and held up one of the two matching table lamps Letty had lent to Belcher's bunch. It would seem that for their Canopic jars, they'd used a couple of real ones!

"I simply don't understand what is going on in our community," said one of the dunce mothers. "It is too deep for me."

But now I turned again, all eyes following. Letty stood near, upstaged, but missing nothing.

"And what in creation have we here?" I called out, staring her in the crown. It was far too ancient for Cleopatra's time. "Here, too," I revealed, "is a fine twelfth-dynasty headdress. You people are looking at solid gold, and notice the workmanship on the carved cobra head. This is a priceless treasure, and was kicking around the outskirts of Bluff City until it fell into other hands."

A creaking sound came from the rear of the room as Mrs. Shambaugh seemed to drop down on somebody's desk top.

I let all this sink in. Letty's mind was whirling. The dunce mothers tried to think. But Miss Fairweather was quicker.

While no one noticed, she'd approached the Princess's mummy. Her hands seemed to move over its wrappings, but I could see she was palming the ruby scarab in one of her hands. "And do not overlook this interesting point, Blossom," she said in rather a stagey voice. "These mummies were often buried with scarabs wound into their bandages as charms to help them to the afterlife."

She drew her hands back. "And lo and behold!" she said. "Here is one now." She reached down to pluck her own scarab from the wrappings and held it up.

"Ohhhh," said all the crowd as it blazed blood-red in the light.

But now Letty came alive. Grabbing the cobra crown on her forehead, she screeched, "We're rich! We Shambaughs are richer than ever! Mother's antique collection is worth a king's ransom, I mean a pharaoh's! Whoopie!"

She danced a little jig in her gauzy getup while all her Sisterhood sighed admiringly. Then she said to me, "You can keep that dumb mummy and that little beetle thing. We've got the good stuff!"

"Ah," says I, "but where did your mama get it?"

Letty's little made-up face went blank. The crowd stirred and moved aside, opening a narrow path to where Mrs. Shambaugh was propped against a school desk. Her awful but expensive hat had slipped over her ear. Triumph and worry were both featured in her face.

"I'll take it from here, Blossom," said Miss Fairweather, elbowing me aside.

"Yes, Mrs. Shambaugh," she said commandingly,

"where indeed did you come by this treasure trove of ancient artifacts which by rights should never have left Egypt? Which at the very least should repose in a great museum for the education of all, if not properly in its tomb?"

"Where she could have got all that stuff is a mystery to me," murmured a dunce mother. "It doesn't seem right." More muttering ensued.

"I trust you purchased these objects from a reputable dealer?" Miss Fairweather inquired. Now I began to shrink.

"Well, I . . ." All eyes were on Mrs. Shambaugh, and for once she didn't like it. She'd clearly bought her ill-gotten goods from my mama, who'd picked that tent show clean.

A vein began to pound dangerously in Mrs. Shambaugh's forehead. She was staring daggers straight at me, just like Letty does. But it began to look like she wouldn't confess to doing business with Mama. Many people won't. Mrs. Shambaugh pursed her lips, sealing them.

"When word gets out that you are the receiver of stolen goods," Miss Fairweather said, "you will find yourself in a court of law, Mrs. Shambaugh. It is a criminal offense." She paused dramatically. "You will serve out your sentence in the State House of Correction for Women as a warning to others," she added, showing no mercy.

The other mothers began to draw their skirts back from Mrs. Shambaugh. She hung on the desk all alone like a beached whale, her head drooping in terror as prison doors clanged in her mind.

At that the room rang with a piercing shriek—Letty's, of course. She turned on her mother. "You have blackened our name in Bluff City and ruined my entire life! I figured you would, sooner or later!"

Letty grabbed off her cobra crown and would have shied it at her mama. But Miss Fairweather jerked it from Letty's hands. She passed it to Alexander, who fitted it back on the mummy's grooved forehead. It was the spitting image of the one the Princess's ka wears, so it was back where it belonged.

"For shame," said the dunce mothers, about the whole thing.

Mrs. Cunningham drew herself up. "Lo, how the mighty have fallen," she said down to Mrs. Shambaugh.

This fallen woman began to whimper, withdrawing a lacy handkerchief from her reticule. "Oh, heaven help me," she moaned. Then, blinking up at Miss Fairweather, "You are an educated woman. Advise me, I beg you. We women must just naturally stick together!"

The ghost of a terrible smile played across Miss Fairweather's lips. "How could I advise you, Mrs. Shambaugh? I who am about to be run out of Bluff City for teaching innocent kiddies suffragette filth?"

The other mothers made lowing noises like cattle.

"Oh, well," Mrs. Shambaugh said, "perhaps I was hasty. Certainly we women must be given what we deserve." She clutched herself. "I mean the vote." She blew her nose noisily and racked herself with sobs.

But Miss Fairweather was unmoved. The spotlight of her monocle fell upon the reticule wedged against Mrs. Shambaugh's big side. With a palsied hand Mrs. Shambaugh drew out the petition. Miss Fairweather waited. At last Mrs. Shambaugh ripped up the petition, and its parts fell like confetti on the floor.

"There is perhaps a way out of this mess," Miss Fairweather remarked, relenting.

We all stood dumb as the mummy, myself included, for I couldn't see it.

A feeble light dawned in Mrs. Shambaugh's bloodshot eyes. "There is?"

"Just possibly," Miss Fairweather said. "You will have to turn yourself into an anonymous benefactor."

"What would that be?" the dunce mothers asked one another. Mrs. Shambaugh was all ears.

"You will have to pack up all these artifacts in crates and ship them off posthaste to the Egyptian Museum in Cairo as a donation. It will cost a pretty penny, but if you return these treasures to their rightful land, your crime may be overlooked. And you had better leave off your return address, to be on the safe side. You can ship back the mummy, too, at your expense. And the . . . ruby scarab."

Beyond the window blinds clouds seemed to clear the sun, flooding the room with golden light. Hope leapt in Mrs. Shambaugh's heart and began to stir in mine. The other mothers were nodding in admiration of Miss Fairweather's wisdom.

"Now, why didn't I think of that?" a dunce mother asked herself.

"But the scandal!" Mrs. Shambaugh whispered, staring in dread at her former troops.

"I am sure your shameful secret is safe with us," Miss Fairweather said. From a handy pocket in her practical skirt she withdrew her grade book and held it high. All the mothers, both the quick and the slow, were reminded that Miss Fairweather had the power of pass or flunk over every kid in the class. "After all"—she smiled—"we women must just naturally stick together." Her gaze swept the room and flitted over the principal. He was back at the door with one foot in the hall.

Mrs. Shambaugh staggered to her feet as a heavy load seemed to drop from her. A weaker and wiser woman, she began to make her way to the front of the room. She might have thrown herself at Miss Fairweather's sensible shoes and kissed her leather-bound hem, but Letty blocked her path.

"I won't have it, Mother!" she stormed, stamping her little sandal. "This stuff is worth thousands, maybe more. Are you going to give it away to a bunch of foreigners on her say-so?" Letty jerked a rude thumb at Miss Fairweather. "Without these museum-type treasures, our house will not be the well-known showplace it is! Why, for goodness sake, everything we've got is old as the hills. Once you start giving it back, we'll be down to the bare walls, and what will be left for me to inherit, I'd like to know?" She paused for breath. "At least we ought to get plenty of credit if we're going to give away a fortune. I am for calling in the newspapers at once!"

Mrs. Shambaugh paused, thoughtfully attending her daughter's words. More thoughtfully still, she hitched her reticule under her arm.

With great speed her heavy hand whipped out and caught Letty a terrific wallop across the ear. Then this massive mother, wordless for once, took Cleopatra by the upper arm, right above the asp, and dragged her kicking and squalling out the schoolroom door.

While Letty's sisterhood stood stunned and clinging to one another without their leader, the bell rang. Mr. Moody melted away.

Miss Fairweather's gaze fell briefly on me. I read in it both gratitude and a couple of unanswered questions. But then she said, just as if this was any ordinary day, "Class dismissed for the time being."

"You can put me down now, Mommy," said Collis to Mrs. Ledbetter.

12

IT WAS AFTER SCHOOL ON THAT SAME DAY when me and Alexander met in the schoolyard, not entirely by chance.

"Well, Blossom," he said. "The Princess's mummy will soon be on the high seas heading for Egypt with a nice assortment of her goods." His fraternity pin seemed to wink in relief as he hitched his thumbs into his knicker pockets in a satisfied way. "And I expect her ka is pleased as Punch."

"Alexander," I warned, "I wouldn't be putting words in the Princess's mouth if I was you. Even if she's followed what we did on her behalf, I'm not so sure she's satisfied. As you well know, she can be very high and mighty—because she is. I myself won't rest easy till I hear approval from her very lips."

"Now, clam up about that, Blossom." A shadow

fell across his face. "I'm sure we've seen the last of
. . . her."

"You can be brave by daylight, Alexander, but
her ka comes out at night. Me and you'd better
stick together like flypaper for the foreseeable future to be on the safe side."

"Humph." He grunted. "You're up to your old
tricks, Blossom. You're just trying to trap the two of
us together in some outlandish situation again. I'm
wise to you."

"You'd better get wise to yourself, Alexander.
However, if you want to take your chances with
the Princess all by your lonesome, be my guest."
Having planted this seed I flounced off. I had a
bone to pick with Mama anyway.

When I got home she was at the table laying out
her cards beside the crystal ball. As she claims to be
a fortune-teller by trade, she was dressed for business. Draped over her humped shoulders was her
old purple washable velveteen shawl with the gold
fringe. Her skirt was the black sateen one with the
silver moons and stars sewn all over it. The
kerchief on her head was tied at the top in a perky
bow. As usual she had no customers, so she'd laid
out a hand of solitaire. But she swept up the deck at
my approach. She can shuffle in the air and do
various card tricks, but whether she can tell a true
fortune is another matter.

"Well, Mama," I greeted her, "you've really put
your foot in it this time."

One of her beady eyes was suspicious while the

other was trying for innocence. "You don't come in here layin' down the law to me, girl," she said, but one of her fingers stroked her sunken cheek in a worried way.

"Funny you should mention the law, Mama, for you've had a narrow squeak today. Mrs. Shambaugh came within an ace of blowing the whistle on you for selling certain items out of a certain tent show."

Mama's eyes narrowed to glittering slits. "The old bag's lyin' in her teeth," she declared. "How much did she tell?"

I sighed. "Not enough to put you away, Mama, but it was a close call. Since when have you been doing business with Mrs. Shambaugh, anyhow?"

"Since I happen to know she collects old junk, and I come across some. It'd been dumped, and you know yoreself I don't like seein' things go to waste."

"Mama, there was a dead body with all that stuff."

She drew in her cheeks and fidgeted. "That nasty thing," she said. "I about dropped my teeth when I seen it, but of course it wasn't real. Them tent shows fake everything. It was like one of them two-headed chickens they put together from parts. I wouldn't have nothin' to do with it myself."

I planted my hands on my hips. "Well, Mama, you were light fingered enough with everything else. Them—those things weren't yours to sell, but

I hope you at least charged Mrs. Shambaugh plenty, because they were real valuable."

Mama settled back and cut loose with a cackle. "I done right well in that department, if I do say so myself. There was a rickety old chair in that trash I wouldn't have busted up for kindling. I asked her a two-dollar bill for it, and we settled at a buck and a half." She thumped the table with a bony knuckle and grinned wisely. "There's a sucker born every minute."

"How true, Mama," I said sadly.

"And then there was a couple of old stone jugs," she said, "both cracked."

"How much, Mama?"

"Seventy-five cents," she said, tears of mirth starting down her long cheeks, "each! The old sow said she was goin' to turn them into—"

"Table lamps." I sighed.

"That's right. And then there was a gold-colored—"

"Hold it, Mama. I've heard all I can handle."

The shades of night had begun to fall during this painful conversation, and shadows started creeping in. "Well, I better close up shop and be about my night work," Mama said. "When you've got a growin' daughter to support, there ain't enough hours in the day."

She rose up and stepped out of her decorated skirt. Flinging her purple shawl aside she tossed on her usual evening outfit, all black to match the night.

Though being all on my own in the evening worried me somewhat, I wasn't sorry to see her go. She was just slumping out the door when I recalled one of the many matters on my mind.

"Say, Mama, do you happen to remember a little ruby-red stone carved up like a beetle?"

She paused in the door with the flat sack over her hump. "Natchurly," she said. "I don't miss much. But I had better sense than to try palming that thing off on the Shambaugh woman. It was nothin' but the prize out of a Cracker Jack box anyhow."

"Who did you . . . palm it off on, Mama?"

She grinned slyly over her shoulder. "The only one simple enough to pay good money for it. Old Man Leverette. But what he'd want with it I couldn't tell ya."

Old Man Leverette? My jaw dropped.

"How much did you take him for, Mama?"

"Six bits!" she said in triumph, and went cackling off into the night.

With no supper in sight I sat lost in thought at the table. Bye and bye I dozed off despite myself with my head propped on my folded arms. I might have slept where I sat through the rest of the night, but it was not to be.

When I opened an eye at some sound, I was looking right into Mama's crystal ball. Then I was awake for sure, because in the ball rose the bluestone cobra with the golden hood, and the Princess Sat-Hathor's face with the kohl-blackened eyes burning yellow into mine. It gave me a terrible turn, for I'd never known that crystal ball of Mama's to pick up a thing.

Then I saw it was only a reflection. I whipped around in the chair, and there the Princess stood behind me. Her ringlets looked new-oiled, and she wore her same gown glittering in white jewels and the collar with more. Her hands were crossed against her breast as if in death, and I saw over each of her long fingertips the gold stalls fitted on them. She blazed in gold and jewels, but they were nowhere near as brilliant as her eyes. I tried to read them, but there's no rushing royalty.

"Flower," she said. "So I was drawn to you for a purpose."

I hung on the back of the chair, transfixed. "Yes, Princess. Your earthly self was located not far from here, where it's been kicking all around North America. Alexander found it."

"A-lek-sander," she said. "Where is he?"

"If I know him, he's home in bed with the sheet pulled up over his head. He lives over yonder in the big house past the barn."

She gave that some thought. "I require his presence," she said. "I will summon him myself." She faded then in such a hurry I half thought I'd dreamt her. Turning up the lamp I sat there dazed through a couple of long moments.

Then clear on the night air I heard Alexander all the way over in his bedroom in the Armsworth mansion. "*Yeow,*" he screeched.

I grinned at the thought of the Princess rising

slowly from the foot of his bed in that way of hers. It was only a couple moments more before he bust in through the front door of my place. His sockless white legs disappeared down into high unlaced shoes, and every hair on his head was standing at attention. I happened to notice he wore his fraternity pin even on his nightshirt, which he was still stuffing into his knickers. He was breathing hard.

"I told my folks I was having a nightmare, which is close to the truth." He gasped. "Where is she now?" His head swiveled around the room.

"Well, she's not far off, Alexander, because she never is."

As if I'd announced her, the Princess grew from a pinpoint of light until she was standing before us, dazzling in the gloom. Alexander swallowed noisily. "What frame of mind is she in?" he muttered, edging nearer me. But we were soon to know.

Her arms uncrossed themselves, and she reached up to touch the gold band around her forehead. "At least my crown has been restored," she remarked, "and one of the lesser scarabs."

Me and Alexander listened respectfully.

"And my earthly self lies out of the wind in its temporary tomb."

By which she meant the Railway Express office down at the Wabash depot, where her mummy was awaiting shipment. "But I am much mystified by the strange and barbaric ceremony of this day." Her awesome eyes grew puzzled, and she fingered her chin in quite a human way.

She had me guessing till it dawned on me she'd been present, though invisible, in history class.

"It is against the gods to wrap a living being, even a small one."

"Oh, well, you're speaking of Collis Ledbetter. Belcher and his bunch were just demonstrating how you ancient folks prepared yourselves for the Afterlife so we won't be so ignorant."

"Hmmm," the Princess said. "And who in Eternity is that mountain of a woman who dared call my possessions her own? She who defiled two of my Canopic jars and could have destroyed my chair by merely sitting on it?"

"Oh, well," I said, "that's Mrs. Shambaugh."

"Surely she is someone's chief wife and a mighty huntress in her own right."

"Well, she's certainly Mr. Shambaugh's chief wife," I explained, "but he buys her them furs, or she just takes them straight out of their store."

"And that wretched girl-child of hers." The Princess's eyes narrowed. "We have ways of dealing with disrespectful children."

"Oh, well, that's Letty," I said. "You're welcome to her."

Alexander stirred uncertainly.

"And the priestess?" the Princess pondered.

"Who? Oh, that's Miss Fairweather. She's a public-school teacher, a kind of wisewoman. Very learned."

"Also deceitful," the Princess pointed out. "She possessed my scarab before returning it to my wrappings in an underhand way. Has this learned woman been my robber too?"

"Certainly not," I said, leaping to Miss Fairweather's defense. "Your scarab was given to her by an unknown admirer named Old Man Leverette. He seems to be sweet on her."

"What?" Alexander yelled at me with his eyes starting out of his head.

I nodded knowledgeably, because of course I knew.

The Princess remarked, "Has A-lek-sander never heard of the love of a man for a woman?"

I decided to let that pass as she chimed a note or two of light laughter. Alexander looked both confused and abused. But the Princess, a creature of many moods, darkened. Even the lamp burned low in response to her, and it smelled like a tomb in the stuffy room. Among the sudden shadows in the house only the stone cobra and her own eyes glittered distinctly. I saw we had trouble on our hands.

"It is not enough," she said.

"Well, now, hold on a minute, Princess," I said fast. "Your earthly self and a tasteful selection of your goods will soon repose in the museum at Cairo, Egypt. That's a proud place like a palace, and you'll get a steady stream of the multitudes to do you honor."

"Pah!" said the Princess as me and Alexander began to cling to one another. "You expect me to lie in state before the multitudes with half my Canopic jars, a single chair, one minor scarab, and my crown? Again, pah! What of this?"

Her gold-tipped fingers fell upon her collar of priceless amethysts. "And these?" She touched the girdle at her waist, which seemed to be made of little snails dipped in purest gold. "And all of this?" She spread out the gold-tipped fingers like spears straight at us while her many precious bracelets jangled a terrifying sound.

"But, Princess," I blurted, "them things didn't make it to Bluff City. They could be anywhere or nowhere by now. They could be swallowed up in years past."

She wasn't interested. "And what of my eight marble vases for ointments, rouge, and fingernail stain? What of my three gold-mounted perfume jars of carved obsidian? Not to mention my bronze pot for the kohl that darkens these." She pointed at her eyelids. "Also two copper razors with golden hands and a jewel-encrusted mirror, the gift of my father, Sesostris the Second!"

She laid out the entire inventory, moved on to her furniture, and wound up with her coffin. Alexander once again shrank to the size of a dwarf. I have felt better myself.

"The diggers draw nearer!" she wailed, and her hands came flying up to shield her crowned head. "Soon they will stand in my empty tomb. They will decipher the wall writings that celebrate my family, not me. They will sneer at my empty sarcophagus, saying, 'What paltry person of unimportance once rested here?' My tomb must be my monument! A museum is all very well, but I will not be taken there in anything less than my full glory!"

She and the cobra's head moved nearer us. "Restore my tomb, or you two will shortly be in yours."

"Oh, gee whiz," Alexander whimpered.

And we couldn't throw ourselves on her mercy, either, because she didn't seem to have any. I racked my brain for a solution or at least a way out. All the while Alexander was staring holes in me.

"What can I do?" I muttered to him. "Her earthly self and her tent-show belongings are being shipped straight to the Egyptian Museum. And all the rest of the stuff she mentioned is long scattered. It'd be a worldwide scavenger hunt. It won't work and we're doomed." I pulled my longest face and meant it.

Still, Alexander's gaze was upon me. He was stroking his cheek and looking very wise for him.

"Wait a minute, Blossom," he said. "What if the Princess's tomb had never been robbed? Then all her stuff and her self would still be in it, waiting for discovery, wouldn't it?"

"Well, I suppose it would."

"Have you told the Princess about your, ah, special talent?"

I froze, and she was listening. You could hear the clicking of her hair beads as she leaned nearer.

"Well, I may have mentioned that I've been known to slip back and forth in time," I said carefully, "but it's no sure thing, and I've never got it down pat."

"Princess," he said, turning to her, "do you happen to know when your tomb was robbed?"

She burned brighter. "To the very night! I rested undisturbed through more than three and one half millennia before those jackals in human form discovered beneath the hillside the door of my tomb. They were rough shepherds, and a lamb had tumbled into a crack in the earth. When they clambered down to save this animal, they found the steps that led below to my sacred precinct."

The room glowed with her wrath. "Under cover of night they pilfered and pillaged. All I had was sold away, and my earthly self began its terrible exile to these ends of the earth." She sobbed, but all her pity was for herself. "It all began fifty years ago this very night."

Again Alexander looked my way. "Fifty years isn't too far back, considering."

"Hold on," I told them both. "Even if I manage to slip back through time to the right moment, how am I going to hold out against a pack of rough shepherds? You should have kept them out yourself, Princess," I made so bold as to say. "You should have showed them your ka and scared the living—"

"Pah," she snapped. "My ka is invisible to everybody but the two of you, who are Sensitives. Those ignorant shepherds were blind to everything but my riches. And they would have laughed at ancient curses. They no longer believed in the old ways of their own people! I don't know what the country's coming to."

But she knew what was coming to me and Alexander if we didn't do her bidding.

"My patience is at an end," she announced. "If you can slip back in time, Flower, I can lead you. The past and the present are a single tapestry to me." She twitched her jeweled skirt in a business-like way. "So let us be off. If you do not serve me well this night, it will be your last. Believe and beware."

My knees like to give out under me. But I was not completely robbed of my wits. "I will give it a shot, Princess," I said gamely. "But I won't go without Alexander."

"Oh, gee whiz," he whimpered.

13

THE LAMP ON THE TABLE LOWERED ITSELF TO A blue flicker, and I stood there trying hard to be elsewhere. I strained my ears to hear distant thunder and tried my best to feel the hot wind of the desert on my face. The Princess, all her patience played out, moved nearer. And I wouldn't turn loose of Alexander.

"Try rolling your eyeballs back," he offered.

"I will attempt an old chant," the Princess said, stroking her brow to remember it:

> *Anubis, god of the body preserved,*
> *Osiris, god of the dead,*
> *Falcon-formed Horus who shows us the Way,*
> *We follow where you have led!*

She swayed as she spoke and for the first time reached out and grasped my hand. I felt the golden nails bite into my wrist and marveled at the fearful realness of her. I reached for Alexander and got a good grip on the top of his knickers. I clung to them both, the living boy and the solid spirit, and our Powers combined. A wind came up out of the grove.

A terrible battering sound at the window made me shriek out in some unknown tongue. An enormous bird was thrashing its big wings against the windowpane—battering and battering with its eye like a glowing bead against the glass. An owl. No, a falcon. The floor began to turn, or the three of us did. We turned and tipped and began to spin until we were light on our feet and the floor slipped easily away from under us.

Then, somewhere below, I heard the front door of our place open and Mama's footstep on the threshold.

"Girl," she said, "where in tarnation do you think yore goin'?" But her voice came from a far distance already, and wherever I was going, I was on my way. And not alone.

The three of us gusted together like an eddy of autumn leaves caught in the winds of distance and time. Though I seemed to hold my breath for miles and years, I remember once seeing moonlight flash upon the Princess's cobra, its fearful fanged face set against the rushing wind. Once, far below us, I glimpsed a black sea tossed with white foam, but whether it was the Atlantic or an ocean of time I couldn't say.

The Princess and I both kept a grip on Alexander, for of course he'd never made such a trip as

this before. I remember how his nightshirt escaped
from his knickers and flapped as we whirled backward through a tunnel of time and how his fraternity pin winked like a star. I remember his terror-
ized eyes and his mouth frozen in a silent scream.

Then we were hurtling above a vast desert. The
sand began to cut our eyes as we dropped nearer
the dunes. It was dark night here, too, perhaps the
last one of our lives. We tumbled then, our feet
skipping over the rills of sand. I remember how the
Princess seemed a bright-painted doll sent skim-
ming by some giant child. I remember Alexander
doing somersaults he couldn't seem to stop and
how white his turning legs looked by moonlight.
We lay at last where we fell. The sand was still hot
from some distant tropical day here in this cold
night, and the wind was knocked out of us.

"Arise," said the Princess, who'd arisen already.
She'd regained all her composure and then some.
Of course she was home and we weren't.

I knew that much as soon as I scrambled up in
the soft sand. The stars above seemed within reach
in the crystal air, and you could see any distance.
Far away below us wound a river, glassy black in
the moonlight: The mighty Nile.

In a patchwork stretching back from it were the
farmers' fields, for they can only grow their crops
in the river bottoms that flood every year to bring
them water and topsoil. I saw the palm trees
around their low dwellings and here and there the
dull glow from a window. On the river were some-

what out-of-date steamboats, though in the fifty years we'd traveled backward they were no doubt modern.

"They call them dahabeahs," I said to Alexander, who was gasping beside me.

"Are they not strange?" said the Princess. "In my day we had lovely barges of gilded wood— cedar from far-off Lebanon." She sighed. "Scented timbers and silken sails," she said in a kind of song, remembering her time. But then she pulled herself together.

"Where we stand is the Necropolis of Luhan," she said, "the city of the dead. We are always buried on the great river's western shore against the sunset, for we worship Ra, the god of the sun."

"The span of our earthly deeds is as a dream," I replied, "but fair is the welcome that awaits us who reach the hills of the West."

The Princess turned her burning eyes upon me. "How do you know these words? They are carved above the door of my tomb."

But not knowing, I couldn't say.

"I thought there'd be pyramids," said Alexander, who seemed to be recovering. Both the Princess and I sighed, for there wasn't any use telling him again how pyramids were perfectly useless in hiding royal tombs.

She showed us the way to hers. It seemed to be just over a high dune. Sand seeped into my shoe tops, and various scorpion-type critters skittered on all sides.

On the far side of this high sand hill the Princess paused. She glanced from side to side, and her ringlets tumbled over her amethyst collar. Then she pointed a golden finger at a place in the sand not far from our feet. It seemed only a gentle fold at first, but we three drew nearer.

There was an opening, down which the sand trickled as in an hourglass. It was just long and wide enough for a lamb to fall into, or a person of roughly our size. But before we entered this underworld, the Princess scanned around us. There on a distant hillside the sand seemed to move in a strange pattern. But as we looked, it became a flock of fleecy sheep. Here and there among them were the orange glow of campfires and the shepherds bearing their tall crooks.

"And which of those lambs will wander away?" the Princess wondered. "And who of those shepherds will be the first to find where the lost lamb bleats beneath the sand? How soon before he lowers his crook and strikes the solid stone of the stairstep? And how soon before he summons the others to break the seals of my door?"

A wind came up to whip her jeweled gown, and she turned a terrible gaze upon me. "Or are we already too late? Am I doomed and you with me?"

She moved forward to the dark opening, and it seemed to devour her in a slow swallow. She dropped softly downward as if she might drown in this dryness. When only her eyes and cobra were still glowing above the sand, she spoke. "My feet have found the first step. Follow."

Then she was gone. Alexander gave me a look of doom, but as in a dream there was no going back. Stepping politely aside he let me go next. I slipped like a jackrabbit down that gap in the sand.

I floundered, too, but then my shoe rang on stone, and I began to descend the steps into the earth. At first I thought any little disturbance might bring the sand collapsing in to bury us. But farther down, the stairs dropped into a hollowness, and my ringing footsteps echoed in a widening place.

Black though it was, this cavern began to brighten from the glowing fire in the Princess's eyes. It didn't brighten much, though, before a sudden hissing sounded behind us. A tide of sand came cascading down the steps, followed by a strangled cry. Alexander had missed his footing and was completing the trip in a series of somersaults. He ended up in a heap behind us, muttering something about being crippled up for life.

But now the entire cave blazed in a lurid glow. The Princess's hands flew up, and the place echoed with her terrible cry. "Curses!" She clutched her head.

Before her stood the door of her tomb with the ancient carved saying above it. But, oh, no, the royal seals upon it were already broken, and the fine door was standing ajar.

"Too late," her words echoed as her elongated

fingers clawed at the air. Then she leapt forward into the darkness beyond the door. I wondered if we'd traveled fifty years back only to find ourselves minutes too late.

"I guess it must have been lamb droppings I slipped in on the steps," Alexander said into my ear, which was absolutely no help.

We trailed the Princess into her tomb, too scared not to. Wherever her yellow eyebeams fell, they glinted on gold and burned in the hearts of jewels.

It was a small room, only a front hall, but the finest of my experience. Around it were life-sized statues of men or gods with the heads of every kind of animal, golden heads painted in evil beauty with ivory horns and real pearl teeth and emeralds for eyes. At their feet lay garlands of flowers, long dead and perfectly preserved in this dry place. The faint scent of blooms withered in the twelfth dynasty perfumed the room.

"Everything seems to be shipshape in here," Alexander whispered hopefully behind me.

But my eye was on the Princess. She was turning slowly, slowly, around. The beams of her eyes fell upon a decorated wall panel. It must have been a secret door, but now it was broken through. Bits of it were scattered over the floor. There in the midst of this age-old plaster lay a tiny drop of blood-red fire. A scarab, dropped in someone's haste.

The Princess split the silence of the chamber with a piercing wail, for beyond the secret panel lay her deathly bedchamber, and now she knew she'd been defiled.

Every jewel on her gown shivered in rage as she flung herself at the broken opening. Yet she seemed almost a human girl suddenly. She even stumbled a little on the stone floor. For a moment she clung to the sides of the shattered panel, and then she plunged into the deeper darkness.

Again we followed her into this place of death, for who knew what might be coming behind us? She stood now in the center of a final room that came to life around her. Blinking in preciousness the greatest treasure trove imaginable unfolded before us.

"Holy mackerel," Alexander breathed. We could scarcely budge for the riches. Every royal need was heaped within these walls. So much grandeur weakened my knees, and I started to settle on a handy chair. But I noticed the fine carved design of winged serpents and sacred falcons across its back and thought better of it.

Everywhere stood rare furniture and the marble vases for ointments. A gilded dressing table held the perfume jars of black obsidian and the bronze pot for kohl, the golden razors and the jewel-encrusted mirror. On another table lay plates of strange fruits: pomegranates, perhaps, and eats I couldn't name, in case there'd be such a thing as hunger in the next world. And everywhere were statues with staring eyes—courtly figures and simple servants all carved from the best materials and waiting for eternity.

Trancelike, the Princess moved in this buried palace. On golden shelves were her royal gowns, powered with dust and delicate as cobwebs. Her hand slid among their neat folds. There glittering on display was the bejeweled double of the white gown her ka was wearing. And there was her collar of amethysts and her girdle of gilded snail shells. Her golden fingertips found the catch of a porcelain box and drew out the identical bracelets and rings that burdened her hands. Her eyes went everywhere, but they smoldered with dread. I saw she was gathering her courage to look at last to the far end of the room. In the shadows stood a gigantic square shape, seemingly carved from a single granite block. It was her sarcophagus.

She turned to it, and then a deathly silence fell as the room burned red with her despair. She neither shrieked nor wailed, but we saw the worst had happened.

The shepherds had been here before us. All four of the Canopic jars stood in a neat row below the granite block. But cast aside was the lid of her coffin, where thieving hands had reached in and ripped it away. It stood at a crazy angle, painted and carved in the form of the living Princess, as realistic as her ka.

She moved nearer this violated place until her golden fingertips rested on the edge of the stone sarcophagus. She stared down as if into a well, and in the voice of doom she spoke. "My earthly self is gone. We are too late."

Too late, too late, too late, her echo answered. *All is lost, lost, lost.*

Alexander's clammy fingers laced with mine.

When the Princess turned to us, we saw only her shape and her eyes. "The robbers will return. My earthly self, even crowned, was a light burden for them, but they will need many hands to bear all my bounty away." Her eyes bored into us. "I am doomed, but at least I will not suffer the rest of eternity alone."

"Oh, gee whiz," Alexander said, barely audible.

But I was trying to think. "Well, when they come back, we'll just have to hold them off," I said.

"Clam up, Blossom," Alexander whispered. "They'll be big guys in a bunch."

But I was thinking now, a mile a minute. "Princess, before you lay a hex on us or anything final, let's us get our heads together. You said these robbers had forgotten the ancient beliefs."

"That is true. Their only creed is greed."

"Well, then," I said, "even if they can't see your ka, they'll be able to see me and Alexander. We're flesh and blood."

"For the time being," the Princess pointed out.

Alexander whimpered.

"So what if me and Alexander made believers out of them? What if they thought we were a couple of ancients passing eternity down here in this

tomb and able to lay a quick curse on the whole
bunch of them. Wouldn't that scare the living—"

"I begin to see," the Princess said, and she
leaned nearer in that way she has. "And word
would circulate among the villages. This necropolis of tombs beneath the sand would become a for-
bidden place. They would shun it and pass the
story down to their children!" Her eyes brightened
with a small amount of hope. But then she darkened.

"But look at you. You are two beings from the
near future, not my distant past. You might surprise them, but they would swat you away like
flies."

"Not if we looked like ancient royalty, well preserved and with revenge on our minds," I explained. She seemed startled at the idea of me and
Alexander as relatives of herself. I pointed to all
the finery on her golden shelves.

"Ah," she said.

"Now, wait a minute," Alexander said. "I'm not
putting on girls' clothes. I'd rather be beaten to a
pulp by shepherds or maybe even cursed."

"But the sexes did not dress so differently from
one another in my day," the Princess said. "Take
off your clothes, A-lek-sander."

"Oh, gee whiz," he whimpered.

How long we waited in that night beneath the
shifting sands I couldn't say. But at last, down in
our darkness, we heard footsteps at the top of the

stairs. Another eternity seemed to pass before we heard the grunt of rude voices, and as the shepherds descended to the door of the tomb, the light from their lanterns filtered in to where we were.

There were a good many of them, filling up the hallway and staring around at the animal-headed statues. We heard their ohs and ahs at all these riches ripe for the pinching. They were licking their chops.

Then their leader showed the way through the shattered panel, and now they were in the Princess's bedchamber. Her ka hung along the wall, invisible to them.

Their lantern flames splashed golden light everywhere as the riches of the room were revealed. They chattered in their foreign tongue, and their hands got grabby.

As Alexander said, they were big guys in a bunch. Their beards were fierce, and their eyes were greedy. They swept off the blankets they wore over their big shoulders and spread them out to heap their plunder on. A sharp sheep smell filled the airless room as they began to go about their business. Quick as a wink they'd snatched up two of the Canopic jars and rolled them onto a blanket.

The head shepherd was just reaching for the remaining two jars when a terrible hand rose out of the stone sarcophagus. An immensely long golden finger pointed between his staring eyes. And then I arose in all my glory from the tomb. There'd been an extra crown for my head, and Letty would have given her eyeteeth for it. My shoulders were bare above my jeweled gown, and I wore quite a fine collar of amethyst stones. My eyes were made up black as night, and my lips were red as the sunrise over the Nile. I was a princess dead these many centuries, but there was life left in me if you were messing with my tomb.

Narrowing my decorated eyes at the paralyzed shepherd, I spoke in a cultivated voice of doom. "Say your prayers, buster."

"Eiiiyeh!" this big thug screeched, falling backward, which made his confederates jump a foot. Then they, too, spotted me. My arms were out, and my ten golden fingertips were spread their way, no doubt sending out curses. Wobbling lantern light added to my effect. Figuring that the English language would sound as weird to them as the ancient Egyptian tongue, I decided to add sound to my effect. I began to speak in a truly terrible voice.

"Put the Bulldogs in the doghouse," I entoned. "Votes for women," I added for good measure.

The shepherds dropped everything and commenced running into each other. Scrambling backward the head shepherd snatched up his blanket of jars and looked wildly around for the exit.

But where the shattered panel had been was now a realistic statue. It stood naked to the waist in a tall double-knobbed crown representing the Upper and Lower kingdoms of ancient Egypt. Its white arms were folded across its chest and bore the two symbols of a full-fledged pharaoh. In one hand was a staff like a shepherd's crook, only gold. In the other was a golden flail. The statue's eyes gleamed at them humanly because it was Alexander.

The rough shepherds swung their lanterns, searching for the missing exit. They grunted and whined with fear. I was still there behind them in my granite grave, sending out curses. Then Alexander's arms moved in a jerky way as if he was just coming alive after centuries. His arms, while spindly, drew up, and he advanced on them, swinging his ancient weapons. It was not a bad show.

The tomb room echoed with their blubbering cries. Only the leader clung to his blanket full of jars, and he was sweating bullets. Another crook grabbed up a convenient chair to shield himself with. They saw the jagged opening behind Alexander at last and enlarged it considerably by trying to get through it as a group. "Eiiiyeh!" they howled all the way up the stone steps and away into the gray dawn.

When the dust settled, there was nothing to show this invasion had happened except two missing Canopic jars, a decorated chair, and the previously pinched mummy complete with crown.

Alexander stuck his own crowned head out through the broken opening. "One of them must have scooped up that red scarab on the way out," he observed.

He looked fine in his pharaoh getup. The crown was a fit, and he didn't seem to mind wearing eye makeup in the interest of authenticity. Around his bare shoulders hung a handsome chain of precious metals and square-cut emeralds. Though he wouldn't take off his knickers, he'd fashioned a pair of baggy pantaloons over them from one of the Princess's gowns.

These flopped down to hide his modern-day high-topped shoes. He was puffed up with a certain amount of pride, never having got the better of a bunch of bigger rough types before. He gave his golden crook a couple of practice swings and smirked with satisfaction.

But I wasn't so sure we were off the hook yet. The Princess materialized somewhat, glancing around. Her glowing eyes drifted past all her treasures to the empty spaces where a couple of her Canopic jars had just been pilfered. And to the spot by the door where the now missing chair had stood.

"Well, Princess," Alexander said, "I guess we gave them something to think about. We can wedge the door shut again and scoop sand over it when we . . . er . . . leave."

"Leave?" said the Princess Sat-Hathor, her eyes hooded.

"Now, listen, Princess," I said, talking fast. "Everything is here except those items and your earthly self which them villains got away with. And they'll turn up in Bluff City fifty years from now. As you know yourself, Your . . . Highness, all that's going to be sent straight to the museum at Cairo."

She was listening, trying to make up her mind if this was good enough. "Hmmm," she said in that way of hers. "I would rather have been found by the diggers resting peacefully there." The precious finger pointed to the looming sarcophagus.

The trouble with royalty is that they're real hard to please. But her glittering glance was drawn now to the jet-black perfume jars on her golden dressing table. She drifted that way. As she removed the stopper, a heady scent of cedar and incense drove out the sheepy smell of the robbers. Then she discovered anew the gem-encrusted hand mirror, gift of her father, Sesostris the Second. Dabbing a little perfume behind both her ears she began to examine her perfect ka-ness in the mirror. Lost in admiration of herself she seemed to forget our presence, but that's royalty for you.

"Oh, very well, you two," she said over her shoulder at last. "I suppose I must be satisfied. Good help is hard to get these days."

A golden hand went out to the pot of kohl to touch up her eyelids. And all the while me and Alexander were back to back, throwing off our ancient costumes to replace them neatly on the golden shelves. And I was stepping back into my regular duds and handing Alexander his nightshirt.

And now we were stealing away through the jagged opening and past the watching eyes of the statues in the front hall. We edged the great tomb door shut behind us and scooped sand against it.

As we began to scuttle up the sandy steps, the

Princess's ka appeared one last time behind us. Doors are nothing to her. The steps were awash with the glow from her eyes.

"Can you find your way back, Flower and A-lek-sander?" she said, less regal than before.

"We'll sure give it a try, Princess," I said from my heart.

But as she hadn't quite dismissed us, we both hung there on the steps, between one world and another. "I promised you a gift, Flower, for your help."

"Oh, well, shucks," I said, "don't trouble yourself, Princess. Glad to oblige."

"It will have to be a very small gift," she went on, "since I am not entirely pleased. A princess never is. Still, I believe you will like it when you get it."

Then her gaze softened, and the narrow space before the door of her tomb was bathed in a pinkish light.

"In my circumstances," she said, "friends are hard to find. I will tell you the truth. In the matter of curses, I had thought seriously of turning the pair of you into a cat and a baboon and keeping you as pets. But I suppose I must let you run along.

"But I shall miss you both. Perhaps one day when you are older you can journey to the museum at Cairo and stand among the multitudes doing me honor."

"You bet, Princess," Alexander said in his changing voice. "And if you're ever in Bluff City again, be sure to . . ." His voice trailed off, and his hand slipped up to cover his mouth.

But behind us the Princess had set up a soft chant:

> *Anubis, god of the body preserved,*
> *Osiris, god of the dead,*
> *Falcon-formed Horus who shows us . . .*

I got a good grip on Alexander, almost a hug, and he gripped back. The steps beneath the desert transformed themselves into a funnel of whirling sand that cut our eyes and sent us swirling. Away we swept up above the dunes into an Egyptian sunrise blood-red as the scarab. Through time and miles we hurtled home, together.

14

ON A CERTAIN NOVEMBER SATURDAY IN 1914 all Bluff City turned out for the annual high-school Homecoming Parade. The crowds congregated early along every major street, and country people came in by the wagonloads from the outlying areas, the weather being perfect for the time of year.

While I had no role to play in this particular event, I turned out, too, making my way down to the Wabash depot where the parade was assembling. There on the Railway Express platform stood a number of crates all labeled for shipment to Cairo, Egypt.

Heedless of them the high-school marching band was milling around in the street, wearing their uniforms of scarlet and silver. Any number of floats were being dragged into position.

Right up at the front was the S.T. & B.F.S. "A-*Nile*-ate the Bulldogs" float to represent us freshmen. Letty's crêpe-paper barge was set on the open bed of a big delivery truck from her paw's Select Dry Goods Company.

Though her makeshift throne appeared to be a kitchen chair painted gold, Letty was already on it, nodding and smiling down at the masses. Her crown, a new one made out of tinfoil, was somewhat tacky, but she held her head at a regal angle and waved her asp at the crowds. Big Maisie, in enough gauze for a circus tent, stood behind her, bearing an ostrich-feather fan. All the other Sisterhood girls were grouped at Letty's little sandals in Egyptian poses.

Several other floats were jockeying for lesser positions, including the Pep Club, Future Farmers, Rainbow Girls, and the National Honor Society, all calling forth applause for their swagged drapings and paper rosettes.

Autumn sunlight played on this colorful scene, and in the midst of it I caught a glimpse of Alexander's blond mop. He was standing all by his lonesome, looking somewhat tuckered out by his recent adventures and gazing about himself. Having nothing in particular on my agenda, I sauntered nearer him.

"There you are, Blossom," he said when I loomed up. "I kind of hoped you'd be here."

I perked up but retained my new ka-like composure.

"We of the Iota Nu Beta fraternity don't have a float, as we're a secret society," he said to explain his standing around.

Nodding toward the so-called Cleopatra barge I remarked, "Of course that rig isn't much to them who've seen the real thing."

Alexander made a little murmur that might have been agreement. He also shot one of his guilt-dripping glances up toward Letty. She was tossing out to the crowd little glass beads which were no doubt meant to represent scarabs.

"The only thing is," Alexander said, "I have lost my fraternity pin somewheres."

"The one with the seed pearl?" I inquired, and he nodded glumly. Along about then my better nature got the better of me. I decided to come clean, never an easy decision. "Well, Alexander, if you're referring to that same fraternity pin you wore even on your nightshirt, I believe I have some clue as to its whereabouts."

He squinted suspiciously at me, so I kept talking. "When we were getting dressed again after scaring off them shepherds down in the tomb over in you-know-where and I was handing you back your nightshirt . . ."

Alexander's eyes were slits now, and his fists were on his hips.

"Well, maybe I just happened to notice that your fraternity pin fell off and got left behind."

"Dad-rat it, Blossom Culp," he barked. "You lost that pin on purpose so I couldn't give it to Letty." Alexander simmered, but believe me, there was relief in his eyes. I know him well.

At this very moment we were interrupted by the

arrival of a new float. A big flower-covered buck-
board drawn by six white horses came rattling over
the tracks. Parting the crowds like the Red Sea, it
lumbered up to cut off the Pep Club and drew in
directly behind Letty's barge.

Standing tall on this new arrival was a large
bunch of prominent Bluff City women wearing
white dresses and pure-silk suffragette sashes. High
above their hats a brave banner was held aloft that
read:

BLUFF CITY WOMEN UNITED FOR THE VOTE
DON'T TREAD ON US
NO TAXATION OR HOUSEWORK WITHOUT
REPRESENTATION

There standing on a pedestal at the top of the float
was the fine figure of Miss Fairweather. Wearing
neither monocle nor scarab she was unadorned
and dressed in her usual sensible outfit. But she
carried in one hand a torch like the Statue of Lib-
erty and in the other a mock ballot. This bold
stroke left the crowd speechless.

"There's Mrs. Cunningham up there with her,"
Alexander pointed out, "and Mrs. Ledbetter."

The dunce mothers were on the float, too, looking stunned but determined, and every member of
the Daughters of the American Revolution except
for Mrs. Shambaugh.

Then from her lofty perch Miss Fairweather
pointed her torch right at me and beckoned me
over. "Blossom!" she called out, "what are you do-

ing down there on the pavement when you should be up on this float with the rest of us women fighting for our rights and an amendment to the Constitution?"

As I could think of no reason, I began to clamber up. Several large womanly hands reached down to drag me on board.

"Do we accept members of the male sex in our movement?" I inquired. And it seemed we did, for now they were reaching down for Alexander. Though he shrank somewhat and looked stealthily around, he allowed himself to be hoisted onto the suffragette float.

At that the flags to November's breeze unfurled, and the marching band broke into a lively but ragged rendition of "The Stars and Stripes Forever." The annual Homecoming parade set forth over the streets of Bluff City.

Miss Fairweather made room on her flowery pedestal for both me and Alexander as forward we rolled through the upturned faces of the crowd. Here and there along the route we received spatterings of applause and some rude catcalls from the men gathered outside the hotel billiard parlor.

"Heads high!" she said to us as we passed these owl-hoots. Then, as we were turning into the courthouse square, Miss Fairweather looked down to me and Alexander on her either side. "By the way, an A for each of you on your Egypt project. It was unorthodox but effective."

We preened.

Then, scanning the far distance in that way she has, she said, "I see by the morning paper that Sir Flinders Petrie has uncovered quite a major tomb in his digging at Luhan, Egypt. It appears to be the burial chamber of a Princess Sat-Hathor of the twelfth dynasty, presumed to be daughter of Sesostris the Second, though the mummy is missing and the tomb has been lightly rifled." Her gaze drifted down to the pair of us and lingered. "A curious coincidence, is it not?"

"I didn't see the paper this morning," Alexander piped up. "On Saturdays I save my eyesight for my homework."

Miss Fairweather permitted herself an ironic smile. "One of your wiser decisions, I daresay, Alexander."

As she'd brought up the subject, I was reminded of the ruby scarab now in the crate and decided it would do no harm to spill the beans about a certain secret admirer.

"Psst," I said up to her. "It was Old Man Leverette who sent you that scarab, Miss Fairweather. I believe he's sweet on you."

Miss Fairweather's head was high. "Oh, heavens, Blossom, I have already figured that out." Though her torch never dipped, the ghost of a smile played across her lips. "A woman knows these things."

"But you can't give that scarab back, because it's being shipped out." It looked to me like she was in a bind regarding Old Man Leverette, who'd now be much encouraged.

"No, I suppose I can't," she replied, and blushed prettily.

Alexander gazed around her fine form at me with his jaw dropped down in amazement. But there was no time for us to contemplate Miss Fairweather and Old Man Leverette as a courting couple before a disastrous thing happened.

Just as we were rounding the courthouse, a terrific clap of thunder assailed us from above. Out of an absolutely clear sky a bolt of lightning sizzled down and struck the float directly ahead of ours, Letty's "A-*Nile*-ate the Bulldogs."

Since the blaring band had deafened itself, it continued to march on ahead. But the truck bearing Cleopatra's barge stopped dead. A wisp of smoke rose out of the crêpe paper just behind Letty's new throne where the lightning had struck. Before anyone could think, orange flames shot up, and the entire crêpe-paper barge began to burn merrily.

Feeling the hot breath of live flame at her rear, Letty screeched and shot out of her throne. Licking flames leapt to Maisie's ostrich-feather fan. Looking up at this sudden torch she screeched, too, and waved it around, setting various parts of the float alight.

By now every one of the Sisterhood girls was abandoning ship. The street was full of gauzy, fleeing handmaidens, and then Maisie hit the ground running. Letty was the last one off, with jewelry clanking and kohl-blackened eyes bugging with terror. She pursued her Sisterhood off down the street, in the rear for once. To the astonishment of the curbside crowd the barge burned down to the level of the truck bed, and a sudden gusty breeze swept it clean of ashes. This freak accident was remarked upon long afterward and never explained.

But I guess I can explain it. The Princess Sat-Hathor had promised me a small gift, and this sudden bolt from the blue, demolishing Letty's float, was no doubt it. Offhand, I can't think of anything I'd rather have had.

We lost the Homecoming Game to the Bloomington Bulldogs, but by and large I was not dissatisfied with recent events. For supper that night Mama served up the absolute last of the rabbit pie.

As I'd put in a busy day, I ate with a good appetite before I noticed Mama wasn't eating a bite. She was only sitting on her side of the table looking innocent, which is never a good sign. As a rule when there isn't enough to eat for two, Mama gets it.

"It's right generous of you to give me the last of this rabbit pie, Mama," I told her, "though I have tasted better." The pastry was stale, and the meat, while still plentiful, was bone-white and somewhat rubbery.

"Oh, pshaw," says Mama with an evil grin, "think nothin' of it. Yore a growin' girl and need yore nourishment what with all the runnin' around you do. But as to rabbit, I wouldn't be too sure if I was you. That old jackrabbit I pried out of a trap was a skinny critter. I had to add some other meat to make that pie stretch."

My jaws froze and I stopped swallowing. "Is that a fact, Mama," I said carefully. "And just what kind of meat would happen to be in this here pie?"

A terrible cackle escaped Mama. "Well, girl, I wouldn't care to say. But put it this way: it is scareder of you than you are of it."

ABOUT THE AUTHOR

RICHARD PECK attended Exeter University in England and holds degrees from DePauw University and Southern Illinois University.

He has written three other books about Blossom Culp and Alexander Armsworth: *The Ghost Belonged to Me*, which was an ALA Notable Book; *Ghosts I Have Been*, which was selected as a Best Book for Young Adults by the American Library Association; and *The Dreadful Future of Blossom Culp*. The Bluff City in these books is Richard Peck's view of his own hometown—Decatur, Illinois—as it was many years ago.

Mr. Peck's most recent books for Delacorte Press were *Remembering the Good Times*, a *School Library Journal* Best Book; *Secrets of the Shopping Mall*; and *Close Enough to Touch*, which was also an ALA Best Book for Young Adults. Mr. Peck lives in New York City.

7 - 9